THE
SPACE
EAGLE

THE
SPACE
EAGLE
OPERATION DOOMSDAY

STORY BY JACK PEARL

*Based upon characters and settings
created by RAYMOND J. MEURER
and developed by
Meurer-Preston-Austin, Inc.*

ILLUSTRATED BY
ARNIE KOHN

WHITMAN PUBLISHING COMPANY
RACINE, WISCONSIN

To adventure-lovers everywhere,
this book is dedicated.

R. J. M.

CONTENTS

OPERATION DOOMSDAY

1.

STOPOVER
IN GREENLAND

THE EARLY autumn sky above Umanak, Greenland, was overcast and foreboding. A scattering of snow-flakes floated down over the vast tundra, settling like fluffy white feathers. From ten thousand feet up, Umanak airfield, the northernmost base of the United States Air Force, resembled a toy village laid out beneath a Christmas tree, dwarfed by the empty wasteland around it.

There was, indeed, a notably festive atmosphere about the Umanak base this third week in September. It was a radical change from the spartan, military environment of the remainder of the year.

Standing on the observation deck of the officers' club on a hillside overlooking the airfield was General Wallace Walker. The base commander gloomily reflected on the perverse fates that brought legions of newspaper reporters, photographers, television cameramen, and other unwelcome visitors invading his domain each year at this time. The occasion was the annual World Grand Prix Air Race, now in its fifth year.

The most advanced aircraft and the leading pilots from all nations were entered in the competition. The course of the race was a great circle approximately following the seventy-second parallel around the North Pole. This year the Grand Prix had gotten underway from Kazachye, Siberia. Umanak was the halfway mark of the rugged sixteen-thousand-mile air race.

To the left of General Walker on the spacious open-air observation platform, a battery of television cameras were focused on the long east-west runway. Noisy spectators crowded against the railing, scanning the murky horizon with binoculars.

General Walker listened to the running commentary of a TV announcer beamed to terse listeners via relay satellites in all parts of the globe. "This is one of the tensest moments in this big race so far. Any minute now, the leader should be making his approach to the runway below us. Leaving the last checkpoint at Barrow, Alaska, the Soviet entry, Vladimir Kozitz, piloting a Russian military jet fighter, held a five-minute edge over his closest competitor, Paul Girard, who is flying an experimental plane, the XY-Fury. There's a note of human interest here, ladies and gentlemen, in case you don't know it already. The XY-Fury was developed and built by the Girard Research Foundation, and Mr. Girard is the chairman of the board of that company." The announcer chuckled. "Just one of the busy and versatile Mr. Girard's numerous activities. . . ."

General Walker grunted to himself. "Numerous activities" was an understatement when applied to Paul Girard. Hardly a day went by without the millionaire whiz-kid playboy providing news copy in some endeavor on the national or international scene.

Heir to the world's biggest cosmetic empire, the House of Girard, Paul had not been content to sit back and loaf on the fruits of his late father's industry. At fifteen, he had been a United States Olympic gymnastics champion. At seventeen, he had been a war hero in the famous Green Berets during the Viet Nam war. At nineteen, he had been elected to the Collegiate All-American football squad. Before his twenty-first birthday, he had been a Rhodes Scholar at Oxford University, had been acclaimed a brilliant amateur painter and sculptor, and had won his Black Belt in judo. There were a score of less publicized accomplishments that escaped the general's mind. Two of the more frivolous of these were his being named one of the world's ten best-dressed men and being voted the most eligible young bachelor in international society's jet set.

The general shook his head in wonder. On top of all of it, the guy found time to administrate the huge and complex Girard industrial empire, including the highly technical and vital work of the Girard Foundation. The first time he had met Paul Girard, General Walker had been prepared to dislike him. The young man was just too good to be true. To the general's own surprise, he had been quickly converted to the "Paul Girard Fan Club" by the amazing young man's modest, friendly, and unassuming personality. The fame and publicity that touched Paul seemed, genuinely, to embarrass him.

The general scanned the thickening overcast to

the west. The correspondents were betting that the Russian, Kozitz, would be the first contestant to touch down on the runway at the halfway mark of the great air race. General Walker had a hunch it would be Paul Girard in his XY-Fury. He would have given odds of one hundred to one on it. And he would have won!

Four minutes later the sleek, silver experimental ship dove out of the mists like an oversize humming-bird. It raced down the runway in a dazzling blur to the thunderous cheers of the airmen lining both sides of the landing strip and the clamoring voices of the newsmen on the observation deck. The cold arctic air echoed with shouts of admiration.

"He did it again!"

"He can't lose in anything!"

"He's a shoo-in now."

Statistics showed that in the four previous World Grand Prix Air Races the contestants who had reached the halfway mark first had gone on to win the big event.

According to the rules of the Grand Prix, there was a compulsory two-hour stopover at the midpoint of the race to enable the exhausted racers to fortify themselves for the final grueling laps across Norway and Siberia. There would, of course, be time compensations made, based on the order in which the contestants arrived at Umanak base. If Kozitz, for example, touched down ten minutes after the front-runner, he would not be permitted to take off until ten minutes after Girard's departure.

Paul Girard held a hectic and noisy news conference for the assembled correspondents and television people in the officers' club. Then he retired to a private room for a light meal and hot beverage with his old friend, General Walker.

"Looks as if you've got it wrapped up, Paul," Walker said over his steaming mug of hot coffee.

Paul smiled. "You never really know until you cross the finish line, General."

"Hadn't you better catch a nap before you take off again?" the general asked.

"Thanks, but I feel great. Must be this invigorating arctic air."

General Walker shook his head and laughed. "You're a remarkable man, Paul. You've just flown eight thousand miles in a supersonic jet through some of the worst weather we've had up here since last May. And you look as fresh as if you had just gotten out of bed. How do you do it?"

"Conditioning, sir. I try to keep in condition."

Top condition was the word to describe Paul Girard. He was the picture of health and vitality, a lithe, muscular six-footer with the reflexes and grace of a panther. His dark good looks put most of Hollywood's leading men to shame, the general decided. Paul was the kind of man every father hoped his son would grow up to be like—the kind of man every father hoped his daughter would marry.

"What's going on in the rest of the world?" Paul asked. "I've been out of touch for the past two days."

"Nothing very exciting. The Russians cast another veto in the United Nations, that's about all."

Paul frowned. "Not the interplanetary traffic control bill, I hope."

"I'm afraid so. Their position was that a space police force could serve as a front for the United States to spy on their installations on the moon and on Venus."

"That's childish and despicable!" Paul said, his voice rising in an unaccustomed show of anger. "Every day that passes, the traffic situation in outer

15

space is becoming more critical. There have been an alarming number of minor mishaps and near misses this past year."

"You don't have to sell me," General Walker said solemnly. "I have the statistics on my desk. A lot of valuable men have been killed, and a fortune in equipment has been wrecked. You wonder how the Russians can be so oblivious to the certain peril of the future."

He took a small remote transmitter from a pocket and pushed a button. "Let's see what's going on in the warm part of the world."

On the wall facing them there was what appeared to be a huge picture mural. The picture faded now as the high-intensity television screen that it disguised glowed luminously. The vivid image of a stateside baseball game materialized. The Giants were leading the Dodgers, five to three. General Walker pushed the button again and the channel flipped. He continued rotating channels until he found a newscast from Washington, D.C.

A pleasant-voiced commentator capsuled the national and international news, giving special attention to the Soviet veto at the U.N. and to the

World Grand Prix Air Race.

"At last report, Russia's Vladimir Kozitz was leading the field in his MIG-XQ-nine military fighter. . . ."

General Walker laughed. "You're behind the times, Mac," he chided the newscaster. He was about to switch off the set when a teletype on the desk beside the commentator began to chatter furiously.

The man tore off the dispatch and studied it. Then his voice broke in excitedly, "Here is a special news bulletin from the National Space Agency Press Bureau in the capital. At 12:35 P.M. Eastern Standard Time, a United States space vehicle of the Pisces Nine class collided with a British space docking port which had been blacked out due to a temporary power failure. Two of the personnel aboard the spaceport were killed, and there was substantial but not critical damage to the British installation. . . ."

On the color screen, the newsman's face looked pale and grim. "There is no way to determine what damages and casualties were suffered by the American Pisces Nine spaceship. At the impact with the space station, all radio communication between the stricken ship and United States' tracking stations blacked out. What little information we do have comes from eyewitnesses on the space station. They report that after the collision the Pisces Nine veered away, tumbling into outer space apparently out of control, its port acceleration rockets dead, and its starboard rockets firing wildly. The United States' Pisces Nine transport was on its way to the moon with a crew of six and a complement of thirty male and female technicians slated to relieve the crew of the United States' lunar base in the Sea of Tranquillity. . . ."

"Good Lord!" General Walker exclaimed in horror. "If that ship is adrift in space, then they're all as good as dead!"

"That's the way it looks," Paul said grimly.

The announcer verified it. "Both Space Agency officials and official spokesmen at the White House are pessimistic about the fate of the Pisces Nine transport and her thirty-six passengers. They are all doomed unless the damages to the ship—which, according to the latest British sources, appeared quite severe—can be repaired by the crew, and unless she can be restored to an earthbound course before her position becomes too remote in space. Her fuel capacity is computerized for a single round trip to the moon with only a small reserve store. Perhaps the President himself has answered the question of the fate of the Pisces Nine with these tragic words: 'It will take a miracle to save them!' "

Paul's voice was bitter. "And that Russian veto today will be their epitaph. The epitaph for the scores, the hundreds, who will perish out there for lack of adequate traffic controls in space."

"What a tragedy!" General Walker said. " 'It will take a miracle to save them,' " he repeated.

"A miracle," Paul echoed thoughtfully. "I wonder. . . ."

"You wonder what?"

"It's nothing, sir. I was thinking out loud."

The general looked at his watch. "Only a half hour left before you take off. Better get down to the field. I'll drive you in my Jeep, Paul."

Paul Girard stood up, took a deep breath, and placed a firm hand on the general's shoulder. "Yes, I must get down to the field immediately. The XY-Fury ought to be ready to go."

"To victory," General Walker said.

"No, sir," Paul answered quietly. "I'm withdrawing from the Grand Prix. I would appreciate it if you would announce it to the officials and to the newsmen. I've got to head back home without delay."

"Withdraw from the Grand Prix!" General Walker was flabbergasted. "You can't be serious! You've as good as got it won. Paul, I don't understand!"

"I'm sorry, sir. No time to explain it to you now. Every minute counts."

Light dawned on the general's craggy face. "It has something to do with that space collision, doesn't it? That's why you're quitting the race and rushing back to the States?"

A sad smile wreathed Paul's handsome face. "Let's just say that at a time of grave national emergency, no responsible American can have much patience with games."

General Walker gripped Paul's hand in both of his strong hands. "I'm proud to call you my friend, Paul," he said, apparently trying to hide his emotion.

2.

THE "BATTLE
OF THE CLOCKS"

The Girard Foundation for Research in Physics and Electronics was a sprawling complex of low, modernistic buildings enclosed by a high chain-link fence in the mountains of West Virginia. The armed guards at the gate waved Paul's low-slung sports car through the gate without checking his identification. Paul parked the car behind the Administration Building and took the elevator up to the second floor. At the end of the marble corridor was an oaken door with gilt lettering: DIRECTOR OF EXPERIMENTAL RESEARCH.

Paul smiled to himself. It was always difficult for him to accept the fact that his young, beautiful, vivacious sister was the possessor of such an eminent title. It was no figurehead title, either. Julie had earned it by her dedicated and brilliant performance in the world of science. Some of the world's most illustrious physicists took pride in the fact that they had worked with Dr. Julie Girard on project developments at the Girard Foundation. Secretly Paul was a trifle awed by his "kid sister," as he jokingly thought of her. Although they were twins, Paul had been born fifteen minutes before Julie—a fact that he liked to tease her about. Sometimes Julie could be an *enfant terrible,* as when she was browbeating her brother with a tirade of intricate equations and theorems.

The secretary's eyes widened as Paul stepped into the director's outer office. "Why, Mr. Girard! Whatever are you doing here? I thought you were up north."

Paul grinned. "I was, Sally. But now I'm here. Is my sister in her office?"

"Yes, shall I tell her—"

"No," Paul interrupted. "I'll surprise her."

He opened the door of Julie's inner sanctum quietly and slipped into a light, airy room with thick carpeting and blond wood paneling. Julie, seated behind her modernistic blond mahogany desk, was bent over a blueprint spread out before her, totally absorbed. A lock of her hair, glossy as burnished copper, hung partially across one eye.

Paul admired her silently for a moment, then called to her, "How is my kid sister today?"

The girl looked up, startled, her hazel eyes wide and surprised. It was like looking into his own eyes, Paul thought. It was the one trait that tied them indisputably as brother and sister. Around the eyes they were identical twins, although Paul's brows and cheekbones were bolder and masculine.

"What on earth?" Julie exclaimed, straightening up in her chair. "Is the Grand Prix over already?"

"For me it is." He walked over and kissed her lightly on the brow, then sat on the edge of her desk.

"I didn't expect to see you for at least another week," she said archly. "All those debutantes and victory parties, you know. You did win, of course?"

"No. As a matter of fact, I withdrew at the half-way mark."

Julie Girard was truly startled. She knew her brother better than anyone else in the world knew him, and one of the things she knew about him was that he was not a quitter. There had to be a very serious reason for what he had done.

All trace of banter gone from her voice and face now, she leaned toward him attentively. "Suppose you tell me about it, Paul."

He told her everything, beginning with the special news bulletin he had heard on the television in General Walker's office announcing the tragic space collision.

"The latest word from the Space Agency," he told her, "is that they can survive for another hundred hours at the outside, assuming that their oxygen-regenerating equipment wasn't impaired by the accident."

"For all anyone knows, they could be dead already," Julie said. "There has been no radio contact from the ship since it happened."

Paul nodded. "I know. It's a chance we'll have to take."

Julie frowned. "What do you mean, Paul?"

He took a deep breath. "Julie, there isn't any way those poor devils can be saved by conventional means. No conventional spacecraft can overtake them and bring them back before that hundred-hour deadline."

She tensed defensively, sensing what was coming next.

"Julie," he said, his keen eyes probing hers, "the only thing that can save those thirty-six human beings from certain death and perpetual entombment in space is the S.W.I.F.T."

"The S.W.I.F.T.!" The slender girl leaped to her feet, her voice high and incredulous. "You can't be serious, Paul!"

"But I am serious."

"The S.W.I.F.T. won't be ready for preliminary tests in space until the end of the month."

"What stage is it in at this minute? I know it came out of Top Security One ten days ago. They must have finished installing the atomic reactor in Top Security Two by now."

Julie turned away from him to the sweeping picture window and stared out at the blue misted mountain ranges in the distance. Finally she said, "The S.W.I.F.T. went into Top Security Three yesterday morning."

Paul nodded with satisfaction. Top Security Three was the last plateau for secret projects at the Foundation. In certain rare projects only one person, the

25

director, had access to the workshop in Top Security Three. The S.W.I.F.T. was a rare project indeed, Paul reflected. The first time Julie had shown the plans to him, his mind had rebelled at the incredible concept. A space vehicle that could approach and possibly attain the speed of light!

Paul Girard had a brilliant mind, and he was as familiar as the average scientist with Einstein's Theory of Relativity. He accepted the Old Master's concepts without qualification, except when it came to the famous and controversial "battle of the clocks" that had been raging for decades among rival experts.

The most startling and electrifying claim that Einstein advanced in his Special Theory of Relativity was that, for an object approaching the speed of light, time would literally slow down. Traveling at half the speed of light—93,000 miles per second—a clock would slow down by fifteen minutes in one hour. At seven-eighths the speed of light—163,000 miles per second—the moving clock would slow down by a full half hour. Einstein's radical theory was a shock to the conventional, orderly scientific intellect.

It had shocked Paul in the beginning, until Julie had patiently won him over. The turning point had come when she told him about a spectacular experiment that had been successfully performed with mesons, high-mass particles with an unbelievably short life-span, about a millionth of a second or less.

A team of California scientists had shot a stream of mesons through a pipe-tunnel a mile long and measured their life-spans at various speeds. As the velocity was increased to fantastic speeds approaching the speed of light, the mesons doubled, tripled, and quadrupled their life-spans. To Julie this proved decisively that time had actually slowed down for the particles as they accelerated to super velocities. So Paul had given his okay for the Foundation to go to work on the S.W.I.F.T. Julie had spelled out the letters. "S.W.I.F.T.—the abbreviation for the great mysteries of the universe that I expect my work will solve someday: Space Warp Infinity Finity Transport."

In the original plans the vehicle had been designed in a saucer shape. Along the way, it had become more of a raindrop shape, heavy in the nose and tapering down to a narrow, symmetrical tail. The fuselage of the S.W.I.F.T. was smooth on all surfaces and made of high-impact, nuclear-forged, fossilized plastic. It could withstand all strain short of a direct hit by a hydrogen bomb. Its unique property of "molecular glide," developed by the Girard Foundation, made air friction negligible. The S.W.I.F.T. was designed to travel in air, water, and space and was hermetically sealed. It could be manned by a single pilot, but there was space for a crew of five. It contained both an oxygen- and a water-regenerating plant. Its main power plant was a nuclear reactor that could push the ship up to speeds exceeding Mach Six in the earth's atmosphere and a cruising speed of approximately 35,000 miles per hour in space. Her top speed in water would have to be arrived at by actual test.

On the drawing board and in most stages of its construction the S.W.I.F.T. did not strike the technicians and scientists at the Girard Foundation as being especially revolutionary. All of the world's leading industrial nations had by this time developed successful saucers or similar vehicles powered by nuclear engines.

The unique property which set the S.W.I.F.T. apart from any existing space vehicle—and from any yet conceived by other researchers—was an overdrive generator developed by Julie Girard. This was based on the mutual annihilation principle of matter and antimatter, a force capable of propellant power exceeding 250 billion electron volts. This generator would be installed in the Top Security Three section of the Foundation's labs by Julie Girard herself.

"Julie, I'll work with you," Paul said. "We'll work around the clock."

She shook her head. "We could never finish it in time. We only have one hundred hours. It's impossible."

"Nothing is impossible," Paul said firmly.

She turned away from the window and put a hand on his arm. Her eyes were concerned. There was a tremor in her voice. "Even if we could do it, there are other things . . . test flights. . . ."

"This would be the test flight of all test flights."

"No!" she said sharply. "It would require days of feeling our way along slowly. You'd have to learn how to fly it in stages."

Paul laughed. "I've ridden everything else in this

world from a bucking bronco to a Taurus Super-X rocket space racer. I can manage the S.W.I.F.T."

"You don't know what you're talking about, brother," Julie protested. "If the overdrive functions as we believe it will, the S.W.I.F.T. will attain speeds that will make every other spacecraft seem to be standing still. If our theories are wrong, if there is the minutest flaw in any part of the ship, the S.W.I.F.T. and you could be atomized into space dust."

Paul grimaced wryly. "It's a risk, but there's only one way to find out. We've got to try it."

Julie blinked back tears. "But not you, Paul. It's not worth the risk."

Paul looked at her solemnly. His voice was gentle but firm. "If not me, kid sister, then who?"

She started to say something, then stopped.

"It's not as bad as you think, Julie," Paul went on. "There has to be a first time for everything. Look at Orville and Wilbur Wright. That memorable day at Kitty Hawk, no one present would have given a plugged nickel that they'd come out of it alive. And if the Wrights hadn't had unshakable faith in themselves and their infernal flying machine, we might still be earthbound today instead of reaching for the stars."

Julie managed a brave smile. "You're right—as usual. All right, Paul, let's go down to Top Security Three and get to work."

"That's my girl," he said, laying a strong arm across her shoulders.

3.

SPACEBOUND

With a black crayon Paul Girard crossed off another box on the big chart tacked on the wall of the lab in Top Security Three.

"Ninety hours," he said grimly. "They've been out there for ninety hours now. The deadline is getting too close for comfort, sis."

Julie brushed a lock of coppery hair from her forehead and grunted without looking up from the delicate task she was performing on the small jet guidance nozzles on the tail of the S.W.I.F.T.

"Don't get edgy, Paul. We'll make it. After this there's only one thing left to do. Install the governor on the overdrive."

Paul frowned. "I still don't like the idea of being restricted by a governor on the engine."

The girl smiled wryly. "I know you don't, brother. And that is precisely why the governor is going on. If I didn't put some kind of leash on you, you'd never be able to resist the temptation to open her up wide."

Paul smiled back. "What's the matter, Julie? Afraid I might disprove your beautiful theory about the space-time warp? I don't mind admitting that I've had some serious second thoughts about over-ruling Uncle Eldon on this project."

Julie sniffed. "Uncle Eldon is a dear, and he's a financial wizard and all that, but if you can't show him that two plus two equals four on paper, he's as blind as a bat."

Eldon Girard, their dead father's youngest brother, was coordinating director of the Girard Foundation and chief of all its operations. A former economics professor and college president, he was a brilliant administrator. Both Paul and Julie respected him highly. It was Eldon Girard who had persuaded some of the world's greatest scientists to devote a measure of their valuable time each year to work at the Foundation. His well-ordered mind had been shocked in the beginning when Julie requested a large allotment for research on her pet project, the S.W.I.F.T. Paul had been tempted to side with his uncle at first, but his sister's impassioned arguments and the impressive charts and statistics with which she had backed them up had finally swayed him to decide in her favor.

"I'm not afraid that you'll prove I'm wrong," Julie went on. "I'm afraid you'll prove that I'm right."

Paul frowned. "Now, what kind of sense does that make?"

Julie completed the adjustment on the last of the jets and hopped lightly off the tail of the ship. She wiped a smudge of grease off one cheek with a sleeve of her once-white, grimy coveralls and slipped the wrench into a large slit pocket.

"Let me spell it out for you again, Paul," she said. "According to Einstein, time is just another dimension like length, height, and width." She picked up a wooden block from a workbench and held it in the air between two fingers and thumb. "Now, it's obvious to us that this block occupies space in three directions—or dimensions—it has length, height, and width. What is not obvious to us is that it also occupies space in a fourth direction that we can't see

or touch. Time. Try to think of the block as an image on a motion-picture film. We have the illusion that the block is a motionless object on the viewing screen. In reality, what we are seeing is a whole series of images moving past the projector's lens at a great rate of speed."

"Yes, yes," Paul complained impatiently. "Stop talking to me as if I were a schoolboy, Julie."

The girl smiled wryly. "You sound like Uncle Eldon now. I wish *he* had a younger mind sometimes. Kids have such open, eager, flexible minds. They're so willing to believe in the miracles of the universe—even if everything can't be checked out on a slide rule or a computer."

Paul grinned and held up his hands in a gesture of peace. "Okay, teacher, you talk. I'll listen like a good boy."

She nodded. "All right, to get back to our movie projector. Suppose, instead of being wound up on reels, the film were a long, endless strip playing through the projector's lens. Now try to imagine that our projector, instead of being stationary, is on a set of wheels moving with increasing speed in the same direction that the film is moving. And in place of the motionless block we'll substitute the image of a boy running along a street. If the film is moving past the lens at thirty-two frames a second when the projector is at rest, what happens when the moving projector reaches a speed half as fast as the film is running?"

"The boy would appear to be running in slow motion," Paul said promptly.

"Exactly!" Julie said triumphantly. "And as the speed of the projector approached the speed of the film, he would seem to be running slower and slower until, at last, when the projector attained a speed exactly that of the film, the action of the film would stop altogether. The image would be frozen on a single frame.

"Mind you, I don't believe it's all that simple in our universe. But it's a convenient frame of reference to use so that our poor human minds can grasp the basic concept, at least, of space warp. Think of our universe, everything that goes on within it, as a series of changing images unfolding on a movie film that is moving at the speed of light. If the S.W.I.F.T. achieves what I am confident it will achieve—a speed approaching, even equaling, the speed of light—

then, for its pilot and its crew, time will pass slower and slower until the instant that it reaches one hundred and eighty-six thousand, two hundred and eighty-two miles per second. At that point, according to my calculations, time will stop altogether. Or maybe it would be more accurate to say that at that point the ship and its crew will be keeping pace with time so that there is no longer any illusion of motion. As in the example of the film and projector, the image would be frozen on a single frame."

"All right, then," Paul said quickly. "Suppose your far-out theory is right—"

"Not *my* theory, Paul," she corrected him. "Einstein was the first one to conceive of the space-time warp."

"Einstein or Julie Girard, the only way to prove it is for someone to climb inside the cockpit of the S.W.I.F.T. and give her full throttle. I don't understand you, Julie. What did you mean before when you said you were afraid that I might prove you were right?"

Their clear, intelligent eyes, so much alike, locked for a moment in mutual defiance. Then the girl's gaze softened, and she laid a hand on his arm.

"Because I like my older brother, even if he can be a stubborn pest at times," she said with a crooked smile. "And I want to keep him around for a while. Paul, you know what happened to the first airships that broke through the sound barrier back in the forties. The jolt shook them apart. We have no concept what it will be like when a craft like the S.W.I.F.T. breaks through the time-light barrier. It could be atomized. It could even—" She broke off abruptly and licked her dry lips.

"Say it," Paul told her firmly.

Julie squared her shoulders and took a deep breath. "The impact could blow it into the vast, unknown sea of time and space, forever out of reach of the world as we know it. Adrift in another time, another epoch. Millions of years in the past or in the future. There's no way we can predict what will happen."

"All right. You win," Paul gave in. "The governor goes on the spartanium overdrive generator. Incidentally, just how much will this governor restrict me?"

"It will hold the ship down to one million miles per hour in outer space," she answered casually. "That is a minute fraction of the speed of light."

"A mere snail's pace," he said, grinning. It made the mind reel—even Paul Girard's good scientific mind. Compared to the top speeds of the fastest rocket space racers, one million miles an hour seemed an incredible rate. Yet it was only a small fraction of the speed of light.

"Let's go into the control cabin, and I'll show you the schedule I'm going to feed into the autopilot computer."

"Autopilot," he said with disappointment. "In other words, I'll just be going along for the ride."

"Not at all. Once you reach the vicinity of the space derelict, you'll take over on the manual controls."

They climbed aboard the S.W.I.F.T. and took their places in the heavily upholstered contour seats before the ship's control panel—a complex maze of buttons, levers, switches, dials, tubes, and television viewing screens. Julie took a reel of computer tape from a compartment beneath the panel and inserted it into the "feed" slot at one side of the autopilot computer.

"You'll attain a maximum speed of thirty-six thousand miles per hour as you leave the earth's atmosphere," she explained. "Within sixty seconds, the atomic engine will kick the ship up to one hundred thousand miles per hour. That's the critical speed when you will shift into overdrive. At that instant, a shield on the side of the atomic reactor is lifted and neutrons and gamma rays are sent bombarding through a miniature cyclotron into the overdrive annihilation chamber. At the same time, the spartanium discharges a stream of ionized particles into the chamber. The gamma rays cause a fusion reaction to the spartanium particles, converting them to heavy nuclei of antimatter. The neutrons from the atomic reactor and the antimatter completely destroy each other, releasing energy equal to the total mass of the matter and antimatter. One hundred percent! Compare that to atomic fission in which only one-tenth of the mass is converted into energy!"

Paul was impressed. "I can scarcely comprehend such thrust."

Julie grasped a red lever on the panel before them. "This is the overdrive throttle." She smiled sweetly at her brother. "The governor will lock it on the first notch."

He laughed. "I get the point." He became serious again. "You know, when you think about it, the principle isn't very different from the old combustion engine. A mixture of fuel and air are fed into a closed cylinder. A spark ignites them, and the explosion exerts thrust against the piston."

"You know the old saying," she said. "From the smallest acorns grow the mightiest oaks—or something like that."

The next five hours flashed by as Julie briefed her brother intensively on the operation of the S.W.I.F.T. Last of all she explained the function and purpose of the masers, the atomic clocks, on the control panel. These sensitive instruments were synchronized with masers in the Top Security Three laboratory. She was confident that this experiment on which Paul was about to embark would confirm Einstein's theory about the slowing down of time at super speeds.

"If I'm right," she said, "the masers in the S.W.I.F.T. will lose about one four-hundredth of a second in twenty-four hours, traveling at a speed of one million miles per hour. That will have to be broken down, of course, because your round trip should only take four hours."

Paul gazed anxiously at the time. "That's cutting it too close for comfort. I wish we had an extra hour or so."

"No chance," she told him firmly. "You can't possibly blast off before midnight."

"At midnight that Pisces Nine will have been adrift for ninety-six hours," he said grimly. "Washington says the passengers can't possibly survive more than one hundred hours."

"You'll make it easily," she said confidently. "In one hour the S.W.I.F.T. will be one million miles into space. You should make contact sometime near the end of the second hour. By my calculations, the Pisces will lie somewhere about one million, nine hundred and sixty thousand miles from earth. In the next two hours you'll have them safely back into the earth's atmosphere."

Paul sighed. "I pray to God you're right, little sister."

At fifteen minutes before twelve o'clock, the domed roof of the concrete silo rolled back, and Paul Girard, clad in a white nylon space suit, prepared to climb aboard his craft. Julie's pretty face was pale and tense as she kissed him lightly on the cheek.

"Good luck, big brother," she said with a lightness she did not feel.

He grinned and rumpled her thick hair. "Stop worrying. Everything is going to be fine."

He ran a hand for the last time along the sleek blue-mist skin of the ship. The nuclear-forged, fossilized plastic had a strange feel, like beads of elusive quicksilver. It was the molecular-glide property of the revolutionary material.

Paul tousled Julie's hair again and got into the ship. He strapped himself into the reclining pilot's seat and fixed his eyes on the masers on the control panel. He counted silently to himself. *Ten . . . nine . . . eight . . . seven . . . six . . . five . . . four . . . three two . . . one. . . .*

His ears were filled with a sound like the roaring of the surf breaking on a beach. Then he blacked out.

All along the Ohio River border between West Virginia and Ohio there were people who were doing late-evening tasks: walking their dogs, putting out the garbage cans, or strolling home from late movies. They stopped whatever they were doing to gaze openmouthed and awed at the night sky as a strange, fiery object whizzed through the air overhead. It receded to a pinpoint and quickly disappeared into the black void.

"What was that?" a woman in a car asked her husband.

"Must be one of those flying saucers they've been seeing in these parts lately," he said.

She shivered and moved closer to him on the seat.

4.

RESCUE
IN SPACE

Minutes after the takeoff, Paul regained consciousness as the terrific forces of earth's gravity relaxed their hold on his body. The S.W.I.F.T. streaked through the exosphere, three hundred miles above sea level, and at one thousand miles up plunged into interstellar space. He snapped off his body harness and levered the seat to the erect position.

He studied the checklist on the clipboard fastened to the desk beneath the control panel. His eyes moved back and forth between the paper and the rows of dials and instruments and flashing lights. So far the ship was performing with the precision of a Swiss watch. The four small TV screens gave a view of space in front of the ship, on the two sides, and, behind it, the diminishing ball of the earth. Soon the earth was just another shimmering point of light in the dazzling myriad of the Milky Way galaxy.

Paul focused his attention on the speed gauge. The needle had touched 36,000 and was climbing rapidly. He glanced at the sweep hand on one of the clocks. Ten seconds . . . twenty seconds . . . thirty seconds. . . . A bead of sweat rolled down his forehead and into a corner of his eye. He brushed it away with his sleeve. His heart was pounding loudly in his ears. Paul Girard was not afraid. What he felt was the nervous anticipation and excitement that all explorers experience when they face a dark, unexplored frontier.

The speed gauge registered 90,000 . . . 95,000 . . . 100,000 miles per hour! The red throttle on the control panel clicked up a single notch as the autopilot computer activated the spartanium matter-antimatter engine. The only indication that the S.W.I.F.T. had shifted into overdrive was a slight tremor, a vibration of the deck plates that Paul could feel through the soles of his feet. He moved his gaze to the overdrive speed gauge. The needle shot up past 150,000 . . . 200,000 . . . 500,000. At exactly 12:08

A.M. it reached one million miles per hour and stopped.

Paul grinned with elation. It was a milestone. He was the first mortal in earth's history to travel at such a fantastic speed. His pride quickly gave way to humility as he recalled what Julie had said. Compared with the speed of light, the S.W.I.F.T. was practically crawling! He could not resist the impulse to reach out a hand to the overdrive throttle. He tried to move it forward, but it was locked fast by the master brain of the computer. Only Julie could alter the programming.

He would have liked to switch on the radio and contact his sister at the Girard Foundation laboratory, but they had agreed beforehand to maintain radio silence for security reasons.

Julie had stated it simply and emphatically: "No one, not even the United States government, must know about the S.W.I.F.T. at this time. It could be disastrous if the secret of the spartanium overdrive engine fell into the wrong hands."

Paul was grimly aware of what she meant. Spartanium was the rarest element in existence. The only gram ever produced lay in the core of the

S.W.I.F.T.'s matter-antimatter engine. It had been delivered to the Girard Foundation by a Russian scientist who had defected to the United States. He had refined this minute amount of spartanium over a period of ten years while assigned to a top security Soviet project for splitting the platinum atom. It was the essence of tons of a special type of radioactive platinum from a mine in Siberia. He had cautioned the Foundation that it might well be the only ore of its kind in the world.

So far the Russians had no idea of the prize that had been smuggled out of the Soviet Union by the defecting scientist. If they did learn of the Girard Foundation's experimentation with spartanium and the development of the matter-antimatter engine, there could be no doubt that their own scientists would eventually solve the riddle as Julie Girard had solved it. Unless the free world could find another source of spartanium-bearing ore, the Soviets would have an exclusive monopoly on the priceless key to the matter-antimatter engine. They could build a fleet of spacecraft similar to the S.W.I.F.T. and, quite literally, control the world. Conventional military spacecraft and nuclear weapons would become as obsolete as the bow and arrow.

No, Paul decided, for the time being the Girard Foundation could not unveil the S.W.I.F.T. to the world.

For the next hour and a half Paul monitored the four viewing screens. The scene was the same on all sides of the ship, it seemed to him—glittering stars and galaxies against an infinite, black background. They seemed motionless, and the S.W.I.F.T. itself seemed suspended in space. It was as if time had stopped, as Julie had predicted it would if the ship broke through the time barrier. But he knew this sensation was only an illusion. They were traveling at only fourteen ten-thousandths the required speed.

When the clocks indicated that he had been aloft for one hour and fifty minutes, Paul began to grow nervous. He should be approaching the drifting Pisces derelict very soon. When the clocks marked off the fifty-ninth minute of the second hour, he became downright worried. Still no sign of the castaways. Had Julie's computations been wrong?

Two hours and one minute! He battled down his rising fear. Then it happened. A red light flashed on above the nose viewing screen. The greenly luminous radar screen came to life, emitting a sharp *beep, beep, beep* alert. He spotted the hazy blip moving into range in the upper left-hand quadrant of the scope.

He realized what had happened. The laser beam from the automatic pilot's ultrasensitive ruby quartz antenna had picked up the lost spaceship minutes before the conventional radar antenna and had automatically begun the S.W.I.F.T.'s braking action. As the retroactive jets cut back the ship's speed, valuable time had to be lost. Already the speed gauge was falling back rapidly from the 500,000-miles-per-hour mark. Then it dipped past 200,000 and finally 100,000. He was vaguely aware of the spartanium overdrive cutting out as the S.W.I.F.T. reverted to its conventional atomic reactor drive.

It was 2:10 on the clocks when the Pisces Nine transport came into view on the TV screen. Ten minutes behind schedule, and he hadn't even hooked up with the damaged ship! Paul was perspiring heavily now.

An illuminated panel began to flash at the top of the control panel, and Julie's recorded voice issued forth from the computer:

"Off automatic pilot. . . . You are on manual now, Paul."

Paul was a skilled space pilot. He jockeyed the S.W.I.F.T. into within fifty feet of the Pisces transport. Her main rocket tubes at the stern had been twisted into what looked like a mass of spaghetti. There was a rip along her port side that appeared to have been made with a monstrous can opener. The ports on that side were all dark. His spirits lifted as he maneuvered around to the starboard side. The ports were lighted, and there were anxious faces pressed against the glass. At least some of them were still alive—alive until their last reserves of oxygen were exhausted. That critical point would occur in just one hour and forty-five minutes. It was 2:15!

He picked up the transmitter microphone that was attached to the digital information computer and snapped out a question: "What is our exact mileage from the earth?"

Almost instantly the answer flashed onto the answer screen: *2,000,110 miles.*

Paul was sick. It was too far out. At maximum speed of one million miles per hour the S.W.I.F.T.

could not make the return journey to the earth with the Pisces Nine in tow before the transport's oxygen was gone. Thirty-six men and women would die gasping for air before he could get them back into the earth's atmosphere.

With a terrible sense of guilt and failure, he nevertheless went about the mechanical task of hooking up to the Pisces Nine. He unfurled the electromagnetic space anchor, directing it toward the stricken ship remotely by little bursts of compressed air from around its circumference. The anchor was a cylinder of carbon steel embedded in a ring of fossilized plastic of the same strength and fiber as that of the S.W.I.F.T.'s hull. It was attached to the underbelly of the ship by a chain forged of links of the same material.

When it clanged into place along the Pisces transport's undamaged side, Paul turned on the electromagnetic current full, firmly securing the two ships together. Then he began the long, desperate journey back to earth. The clocks read 2:30. He was a full thirty minutes behind schedule.

Here in interstellar space, he ran the S.W.I.F.T. up to her maximum speed of one million miles per hour in far less time than it had taken on the first leg of the journey.

With every passing minute, his frustration grew as his gaze traveled helplessly from the speed gauge to the clocks, to the image of the Pisces Nine on the viewing screen, and, finally, to the red throttle handle of the spartanium overdrive engine. If only Julie had not restricted him by putting the governor on the overdrive.

A reckless thought struck him. The governor consisted of a dual valve that controlled the rate of flow of neutrons and gamma rays from the atomic engine and ionized particles from the spartanium reactor into the annihilation chamber. Its action was regulated by energy from the nuclear batteries stored in the stern of the ship. He reasoned that Julie must have made some safety precautions in the event that the governor valves developed a defect and failed to operate. The logical thing was that she had fed directions into the autopilot computer to allow for manual operation of the overdrive throttle *if* the governor failed. If he was right, all he had to do now was to short-circuit the cables running from the batteries to the governor, and the brake on the overdrive would be off! It was a wild chance, but it was his only chance.

He opened the drawer of the desk under the control panel and searched through the stack of charts and blueprints it contained until he found a diagram of the S.W.I.F.T.'s wiring system. It was 2:45. There was not a moment to waste!

It took him another fifteen minutes to locate the proper cable leading from the nuclear batteries to the ship's twin engines. At least he hoped that it was the right cable. It was as thick as his middle finger, bound in blue-and-yellow striped casing. If it was the wrong one, the whole ship might blow up in his face. There was only one way to find out, Paul knew. He found a pair of insulated shears in the tool bin and cut it!

There was no appreciable change in the behavior of the craft. That was something, anyway. He breathed out in relief. Returning to the pilot's seat, he sat down and reached for the red handle and tried to advance it. It held firm. His heart sank. He strained at it. It seemed to give a little, and his heart beat faster. A little more push. This time it moved forward a notch.

Almost afraid to look, he turned his eyes on the overdrive speed gauge. The needle moved up toward the 1,500,000-miles-per-hour mark! He sank back in the seat weakly. Now they would make it.

He fed some instructions and computations into the autopilot computer and switched the controls off manual. The infallible mechanical pilot would implement the necessary braking maneuver as they neared earth and bring them down safely into the atmosphere. The passengers in the stricken Pisces Nine would breathe the good air of the earth again and live to tell their tale of being shipwrecked in the dark sea of space.

He frowned. There was one thing that he and Julie had not considered in the excitement of getting ready for the S.W.I.F.T.'s rescue mission. There would be thirty-six eyewitnesses who would spread the incredible story of their miraculous rescue by a strange, unidentified spacecraft that was shaped like a raindrop and traveled through space at a speed that was unbelievable.

It would be the first crack in the wall of secrecy Julie Girard had put up around the development and construction of the S.W.I.F.T. Now the public, the government, the newspapers, the whole world, would not rest until the mystery was solved. Paul had a hunch that the days ahead would be trying for him, for Julie, and for the Girard Foundation.

The S.W.I.F.T. eased gently into the earth's atmosphere at 3:58 A.M. with the Pisces Nine swinging in an arc below it from the electromagnetic anchor. Back in the earth's gravity field, the big space transport was an enormous dead weight, but the anchor held fast, and the S.W.I.F.T. was a little giant of super power.

Paul deposited his burden gently in a desolate plain in Kansas in an attempt to throw the bloodhounds off the scent once the word flashed around the world that the space castaways were safe.

Then, without waiting for a thank-you, he gunned the S.W.I.F.T. back toward West Virginia. It was still and dark at the Girard Foundation when he settled the S.W.I.F.T. back into her silo berth inside the domed roof of the Top Security Three laboratory.

Minutes later, Julie flung herself into his arms and hugged him. Her cheeks were wet, but Paul pretended he did not notice.

"I was beginning to think . . ." she began in a choked voice.

"Hush, little sister," he said, grinning. "It was a dream flight all the way." He hesitated and added wryly, "Well, maybe not *all* the way."

He told her about the time error and how he had saved the day by shorting out the governor.

Julie paled. "What a fool I was to put on that governor! It could have meant the death of all those people." She hung her head. "I'm ashamed of myself for not trusting your judgment. I might have known you wouldn't do anything foolhardy."

He laughed. "Like trying to break your so-called time barrier? No, not when thirty-six innocent people's lives depended on me." He tipped up her chin with one hand and said firmly, "But next time watch out, my girl."

5.

THE BIRTH
OF THE SPACE EAGLE

THE PRESIDENT of the United States sat behind his big desk, frowning at the newspapers scattered in front of him. Pacing up and down in front of the desk were the director of the Central Intelligence Agency, the chief of the Federal Bureau of Investigation, and the Secretary of State.

They all looked toward the door as the President's news secretary burst into the room.

"The reporters are demanding a news conference, sir," he said with agitation. "What shall I tell them?"

The Chief Executive grunted. "Tell them anything you want. You know as much about this business as I do."

When the news secretary had left, the President banged his fist on the desk. "Look at this headline:

'Shipwrecked spacemen rescued by saviors from another planet!' Do any of you actually believe that?"

"No, Mr. President," said the director of the CIA. "But the men and women who were in that wrecked Pisces Nine transport believe it. I was present when Captain Rose was interrogated. He said this craft had to be from another world. It traveled at super speeds far faster than our fastest space racers."

"Yes," the Secretary of State agreed. "And last night the Air Force checked out hundreds of reports of flying saucers sighted in the central coastal states. And at midnight, and again at four o'clock this morning, the North American Air Defense Command sighted an unidentified flying object on its radar. Each time, our space rocket jet fighters took out after them, but it was no use. The UFO simply vanished in a fiery vapor so brilliant that it temporarily blinded our pilots."

"It's outlandish!" the President said. "What am I going to tell those reporters? What am I going to tell the world?"

"I'd like to make a suggestion, sir," the FBI chief said.

"I'm open to any suggestion that will solve this

61

puzzle. Go ahead. Let's have it."

The chief spread a map of the United States on the President's desk. There was a circle drawn with a red crayon around an area that took in portions of Pennsylvania, Maryland, Virginia, Kentucky, Ohio, and all of the state of West Virginia.

"I got this map from the Air Force files," he explained. He followed the round crayon mark with his forefinger. "Suppose this circle is a wheel. Now let's find the hub." He sketched in a half-dozen intersecting spokes with a black crayon and drew a star at the point where they all met in the circle's center.

"For months now," he went on, "the section of the country inside this circle has reported more UFO sightings than any other section of the United States. Last night, too, the heaviest concentration of reports about that strange spaceship came from the same vicinity."

"What are you driving at?" the President asked.

The FBI chief drew a small **x** a little to the right of the wheel's hub. "Just that this is the site of the Girard Foundation's experimental laboratories. Isn't it possible that there is a direct connection between all the recent saucer sightings—as well as the mystery ship that saved our spacemen last night—and the Girard Foundation?"

The President's face darkened. "Are you suggesting that the Girard Foundation is playing some kind of hanky-panky behind the government's back? Why, that's ridiculous! The United States has managed to keep its lead in the space race largely through the great contributions that the Girard Foundation has made to our military and scientific arsenal."

"That's true, sir," the CIA director put in politely. "But you will admit that it is also a very, very independent organization. You can never get straight answers from any of the Girard people until they decide they want to give you the answers. You recall that trouble we had with Dr. Julie Girard a few years back over that cosmetic project that the House of Girard began working on during the war in Viet Nam?"

"The one to help veterans who had been disfigured by wounds and napalm burns? Yes, I remember."

"The Girards never would release the formulas of the medicines they used or the secret of the treatments to the veterans' hospitals. Their own staff of technicians traveled from hospital to hospital administering to the wounded."

The President began to chuckle. "Yes, that's right. Then, after our boys recovered, no one ever heard about the miracle process again. 'Instant plastic surgery' they used to call it. They claimed it would be too dangerous if they let the medical profession use it commercially. Every crook in the underworld could have his face changed at will. Oh, yes, the Girards are independent, all right."

"Stubborn is the word," the CIA chief said. "Our people could never get anywhere with them."

"And that playboy who runs the whole works is the worst of all," the FBI chief agreed moodily.

"Paul?" the President said fondly. "Don't let that boy fool you. He's a remarkable young man. I've known Paul and Julie Girard since they were young enough to bounce on my knee. Their father was my roommate at college, you know."

The Secretary of State interrupted eagerly. "That may be the answer, Mr. President. Maybe you could have a friendly chat with Paul Girard, off the record. If the Girard Foundation did have anything to do with that mysterious spaceship that saved the

Pisces Nine and its passengers, you may be able to get him to confide in you as a friend. You can make him understand the embarrassing spot this unexplained incident has put us in."

The President looked around at the anxious faces about his desk, and he sighed. "Well, I suppose it's worth a try. I'll get in touch with Paul Girard at once."

Paul Girard listened in attentive silence as the President patiently explained his problem in a quiet, reasonable way.

"All this furor about an alien spaceship that can travel at fantastic speeds and penetrate the air defenses of the United States at will has the people worried. And our enemies will get cocky. They'll begin to think that if one little ship can fool NORAD and SAC, then maybe their bombers and missiles will have a chance, too. I've got to come up with some answers, Paul, and fast. The public and the press will lose faith in me and the government if I can't give them some reasonable explanation of what that mystery spaceship was and where it came from."

It was a strong appeal, and Paul felt himself being backed into a corner. He liked the President and respected him. He understood and sympathized with all that the President had said. Still, he had vowed to Julie before he left for Washington that he would not reveal anything at all about the S.W.I.F.T. no matter how long or how hard he was questioned.

"I wish I could help you, sir," he said evasively, "but I can't."

The President studied the handsome young man across his desk with keen eyes. "I thought possibly your sister Julie was involved in some new project. We both know how that girl works, Paul. Why, the security measures out at the Foundation labs are stricter than some of the government's top-security precautions."

Paul met his gaze steadily. "You can depend on it, sir, that if Julie is working on anything that could prove beneficial to the United States, you will be the first one to know about it, when the time is right."

The President leaned across the desk, and he was not smiling. "Paul, this isn't like you. You haven't given me a straight answer since we started to talk. I think the CIA and the FBI are right. You are hiding something from me."

Paul's eyes fell. "I'm sorry you feel that way, sir. I would think you knew me well enough to trust me."

"I would think you knew me well enough to trust me!" the President snapped back.

It was a telling blow. For a moment Paul could not speak. He knew now that the President was right. He would have to break his vow to Julie. It was better to confide in the President than to have government agents swarming all over the Girard Foundation. He took a deep breath.

"All right, Mr. President," he said tensely. "I'll tell you what you want to know."

Paul kept his word. He told the President all about the S.W.I.F.T., beginning with the defecting Russian scientist who had brought the gram of precious spartanium to the Girard Foundation. He impressed on the President that as far as they knew, the only source of the platinum ore from which spartanium was refined lay inside the Soviet Union.

"If the secret of the S.W.I.F.T.'s spartanium matter-antimatter engine falls into Russian hands before we locate another source of this rare ore," he said, "then the Russians will have the power to control the world."

The President understood perfectly. "You and Julie are right, Paul," he agreed. "For the present, the secret of the S.W.I.F.T. will be in the Foundation's keeping. If it is turned over to an official government agency now, it will be fair game for every Russian agent in this country. The secret of spartanium might leak out to them, just as the secret of the atom bomb leaked out to the Russians after World War Two. It was bad enough to have the atom secrets stolen, but to have this secret stolen would be fatal to our security—to the security of the free world."

"I appreciate your attitude, Mr. President," Paul said with gratitude.

The President sighed. "As for the rescue of the wrecked space transport the other night, I'll let the Intelligence boys worry about making up some half-way logical story to give to the press. We can say that the damaged ship was towed in by a conventional force, that the passengers in the Pisces Nine were suffering from hallucinations from lack of oxygen. All those people are top-security risks. They'll back us up if we tell them it's vital to the safety of the nation."

Paul began to relax. "Thank you again, sir. You won't regret your decision. It goes without saying that the Girard Foundation will transfer the project to the government at the proper time."

"I know that, Paul." The President got up and came around the desk. A tall, lanky man, he towered over Paul's chair. An idea had been cooking in his mind for some days now, ever since the Russians had vetoed the resolution for a United Nations space police force to regulate and conduct interplanetary rocket traffic.

"Paul," the President began seriously, "no one in this nation can ever question the patriotism of the Girards. There were Girards fighting to build and defend this country as far back as the French and Indian Wars. They fought in the Revolution. They helped push the frontier westward. Girards died at Gettysburg, on San Juan Hill, on the Marne and on the Somme in World War One. Your dad won the Silver Star for his heroism in the Ardennes Forest, and your Uncle Eldon did his bit on Red Beach in World War Two. You, yourself, were wounded and decorated in Viet Nam. What I am going to ask you now is that you volunteer to put yourself on the firing line, as it were, once more."

Paul blinked up at the tall, gray-haired man. "I don't understand, sir. What firing line?"

"The frontiers of space need patrolling, just as our continental frontiers did generations ago. Did you know that your great-great-grandfather was a United States Marshal in the Oklahoma territory when the West was really wild?"

"I do, indeed, sir," Paul said with pride. "His six-guns are displayed in a showcase in the Colt Fire-arms Museum. There are nine notches on them."

"Yes, I know." The President sat down on a corner of his desk and smiled. "The frontier never would have been tamed without men like Cyrus Girard. The frontier of space may never be tamed without men like him. Right now out there it's as lawless and undisciplined as the territory beyond the American frontier used to be more than one hundred years ago."

He frowned darkly. "If the Russians have their way, it will remain untamed. You know they vetoed a U.N. plan for a space police force?"

"Yes, sir."

The President rubbed his palms together. "Well, I have just about decided that the United States has to do something about it. I want to set up a Spatial Intelligence Agency to protect our growing interests within the solar system. And beyond the solar system, when that time comes."

"That sounds fine to me," Paul said. "It would be like the CIA and the FBI—only airborne."

"Yes, but it would be something more. As I see it, a space agent would have to be more of a frontier marshal. As I said, there is a total lack of law up in space at this time, except for a few loose treaties outlawing the moon and the planets as sites for military operations. And even those can't be truly enforced, because there are no interplanetary policemen."

"I see what you mean, sir." Paul was suddenly on his guard. "But what has it got to do with me, Mr. President?"

The President gave it to him squarely. "I want to appoint you as the chief of the United States Spatial Intelligence Agency, as well as its first operative. Will you do it?"

Paul Girard offered a dozen reasons why it was impossible for him to accept the great honor. There were his countless responsibilities and burdens as chairman of the board of the House of Girard Cosmetics and Chemical Company and its worldwide chain of beauty salons, Glamor Unlimited, as well as the Girard Foundation. He pointed out, too, that his reputation as a polo-playing, scuba-diving, speed-racing member of the international jet set hardly went with the dignity required by the important government post the President was offering to him.

"I think it's the perfect background for the chief of a secret intelligence agency," the President disagreed. "Think of the camouflage it will give you. No one would suspect that you were a government agent. Your playboy activities give you a chance to jet to all parts of the world on missions for the United States, and no one, especially the Russians, will ever be the wiser."

"I don't know, sir." Paul shook his head to clear it.

The President pressed on. "Paul, you are a very special man, physically, athletically, intellectually. Your special talents, your social position, make it possible for you to make a vital contribution to the security of this nation. You might be the one man who can tip the scales in our favor in the cold war with the Communist world. The stakes are high, Paul. Freedom!"

It was all very clear to Paul then. Everything that he was, everything that he owned—the Girard Foundation, the House of Girard, all of it—he and his family owned by the grace of God and the freedom that was every man's birthright in the United States.

He got up and stood tall and erect before the man sitting on the edge of the desk. "Mr. President," he said solemnly, "I accept with honor."

The President grinned and extended his hand. His grip was firm and warm. "In the future, the Spatial Intelligence Agency will be expanded, of course. But for the present, Paul, you are it, the whole operation. It's not an easy assignment. You're in somewhat the same position your great-great-grandfather was in when the government sent him into the Indian territories with only his six-guns on his hip to write the law. You're a little better off, though. Instead of a pair of guns, you've got the S.W.I.F.T."

Paul smiled weakly. "That will give me a lot of muscle power for a one-man agency."

"For the time being, you will be responsible to no one in the government other than the President of the United States. This must be kept top top secret. . . . Let's see, we'll have to give you a code name and code number for positive identification when you want to contact Washington."

He thought a moment. "How about seventy-six sixty for the number? Short for 1776—the Spirit of '76 and the symbol of American independence. And short for 1960, the year the first American astronaut broke through the frontier of space. Your code letters will be the symbols of two of the many things that make our nation so great. IA—Independence and Achievement!"

"I like that, sir," Paul said.

The President thoughtfully scratched his chin with a fingernail. "Now what about your code name?" He picked up a newspaper clipping from his desk. "You must have read this story given to the newspapers by one of the technicians aboard that wrecked space transport. She said that they had all given up hope when you arrived. She describes the mystery ship that rescued them as 'looming up out of the darkness of space like a great eagle.' I like that, Paul; don't you? The Space Eagle!"

"It makes me sound like some sort of superman," Paul said with modesty, "but if you like it, I don't object."

"That's it, then, Paul," the President said. "Wherever you are, any part of the globe or out in space, night or day, all you have to do is to dial my number and give the password: 'Space Eagle here—seventy-six sixty.' I won't keep you waiting, my boy. You can depend on it."

6.

THE EAGLE'S CLAWS

BACK AT THE Foundation, Paul described the outcome of his visit with the President to Julie. For some years he had known that his sister's temper was as fiery as her coppery hair, but he had never seen her this angry before.

"You don't fool me, brother," she scolded him. "This is just a fancy excuse for you to indulge your childish whims and to ignore your responsibilities to the business and the Foundation. Imagine, a grown man playing cops and robbers in outer space!"

Usually when Julie was in one of her moods, Paul would wait until she ran out of steam. Then he would tell her how pretty she looked when she was angry and joke about her terrible temper scaring away all of her boyfriends. The two of them always ended up laughing like children.

This time it was different. Paul was in no joking mood. He walked over to Julie, who was standing by the big window behind her desk, and gripped her arms firmly.

"Now, you listen to me, little sister," he said in a severe voice. "When you talk about responsibilities, just stop and think for a moment what the biggest responsibility is that you and I have as Americans. Our first responsibility is to our country. It's been that way since 1776, Julie. I didn't accept this job because it sounded like fun. I accepted it because it was my clear duty."

Their hazel eyes locked, and abruptly all the anger drained out of the girl's pretty face. She looked ashamed.

"I—I'm sorry, Paul," she said in a low voice. "I should have known that was the reason. Forgive me."

"Of course I forgive you. And don't worry about the House of Girard and the Girard Foundation. I promise I won't neglect my duties to them."

Julie smiled. "Of course you won't." Her eyes

brightened eagerly. "Do you know what your first official act as chief of the Spatial Intelligence Agency is going to be?"

Paul's forehead creased. "No, what?"

"You're going to deputize Dr. Julie Girard as your first deputy."

He laughed. "You must be joking!"

"No, Paul, I couldn't be more serious. Listen, I'm not going to have my only brother chasing around through space after spies and interplanetary badmen unless he's thoroughly prepared."

"Prepared?" Paul blinked in bewilderment. "I'll have the S.W.I.F.T. on my side. That's a pretty good start, I'd say."

"You're right. But the S.W.I.F.T. is only a beginning. Before you go running off on your first assignment, you're going to be outfitted by the Girard Foundation."

"Outfitted?"

Julie grinned mysteriously. "You just leave it to me. Look, Paul, you've had a hectic week. Why don't you run down to Paradise Valley for a few days and rest up. Mother says she hasn't seen you in months."

Paul rubbed his jaw thoughtfully. He *was* weary. "You're right, sis," he said. "I will go spend a few days with Mother. It will take the edge off."

As he was leaving the office, he turned to her with a raised eyebrow. "I can hardly wait to find out just what all this 'outfitting' is that you have in mind."

She patted his shoulder. "In due time, brother. In due time."

Paradise Valley lay between two blue-hilled mountain ranges in central Kentucky. The Girard ancestral home, a grand old mansion in the nineteenth century Southern Colonial style, stood at the head of the valley. Surrounding it and running the length of the valley behind it were a thousand acres of untouched forest. The home and property had come originally from Paul's mother's family, the Fontaines, who had been breeders of fine horseflesh since before the Civil War. The Girard and Fontaine stables had always been, and still were, the source of most of the world's finest racehorses.

Emilie Girard, well in her fifties, was a living testimony to the wonders of Girard cosmetics and its Glamor Unlimited beauty salons.

"You get lovelier every time I see you, Mother," Paul said as he kissed her cheek upon his arrival at Paradise Valley. "All it would take would be some gaudy makeup and one of those new dresses the young girls are wearing these days, and you could pass as a jet-set debutante."

"That's very flattering, Paul," Emilie Girard said with a smile. "But I have no desire to look like anything but what I am, a fifty-five-year-old mother of two wonderful grown children." She pretended to frown. "Only I'd think they were even more wonderful if they would settle down and let me become a grandmother."

Paul laughed. "You're the wonderful one, Mother. Don't worry, one of these days our little Julie is going to surprise you. She'll meet some dashing scientist with a brain that's even bigger than hers, and they'll live happily ever after and raise a family of little computers."

"Oh, Paul, you are awful to tease your sister like that." Emilie Girard laughed heartily, nevertheless.

Samuel Aarons came around the corner of the house at that moment, and he and Paul had a happy reunion. Paul was over six feet tall and had a muscular physique, but beside the huge, smiling Negro he looked like a boy.

Samuel was ageless in his appearance. No one knew how old he was, in fact, but he had been working with the Fontaine family as estate manager since Emilie had been a young girl. He had a glistening bald head which he shaved daily as part of the strict mental and physical discipline he had practiced after a near-tragedy in his youth. Samuel had seen a man beating a helpless horse at a state fair. In a fit of rage, Samuel had almost killed the man. He would have gone to jail for life if Jacob Fontaine had not used all of the influence and respect he enjoyed in the state to get Samuel released on parole in his custody. Soon after that Samuel had become a serious student of the oriental and Hindu philosophies of restraint and nonviolence.

As a boy growing into manhood, Paul had spent more time with Samuel in the outdoors than he had spent with his family. They had hunted and fished and ridden together. And they had talked long into the night sitting around campfires deep in the wilderness. It could truthfully be said that Paul's high ideals, strong character, and physical and moral fitness were due to his close association and friendship with Samuel Aarons.

For the next three days, Paul and Samuel happily renewed their friendship and did the things they had not done together for so long. As the responsibilities of his business and social life had increased year after year, Paul's visits to Paradise Valley had become less and less frequent. Now, on the last day of his visit, it was with sincere sadness and regret that he said good-bye to his mother and Samuel and flew back to the Girard Foundation.

Julie was excited and pleased to see him. "We'll go right down to Top Security Three," she said impatiently without even giving him a chance to catch his breath. "I have some interesting things to show you."

Paul was amazed at what his sister had been able to accomplish in three short days. The S.W.I.F.T. had been equipped with laser cannons in the nose and tail. Julie described them.

"The range and direction are automatically set by radar. All you do is push the button and *wham!* These laser beams can drill a hole two feet in diameter through three feet of cadmium steel in the blink of an eye."

Paul smiled. "I'd hate to get in the way of anything like that."

"The Space Eagle's enemies won't like it very much, either," she said. She pointed out another weapon installed in the nose. "Or if you prefer to take prisoners, this rocket projectile launcher will be more to your liking. The projectiles are armor-piercing and heat-sensing. Their guidance systems can find a thin dime out in space by zeroing in on the solar heat it reflects. They're filled with a fast-acting anesthesia."

Paul whistled in awe. "What other wonders have you whipped up for me?"

"I didn't actually have to 'whip up' these gadgets overnight," Julie confessed. "Most of them are things the Foundation has developed in the past. These models came from the Top Security Three research vault. It was just a matter of making a few fine adjustments to get them into working order."

Paul picked up a small gas-powered pistol from a display table. "Now, what is this little toy?"

Julie pointed to a corkboard at one end of the

room. "Fire away and see for yourself."

Paul aimed the pistol and pulled the trigger. There was a soft *pop!* like the sound of a bottle being uncorked. They walked to the end of the room and examined the board. Embedded in the cork was a small dart made of silver plastic. Paul's eyes widened as he studied it. "Why, it looks like. . . ."

"An eagle's talon," Julie finished it for him. She beamed proudly. "Tranquilizer darts. They'll put a man to sleep instantly for four hours. I thought casting them in the shape of an eagle's talon was a cute touch, don't you? A talon gun, and the darts are 'talons' of the Space Eagle."

Paul put an arm around her shoulders and laughed warmly. "It's a cute touch, all right. You know, underneath that mask of graph paper and transistors and higher mathematics there is a real, live girl."

Julie blushed prettily. "You think it's silly! I'm sorry."

"Not at all," he assured her. "The more I think about it, the better I like it. Seriously, it's a known fact that the criminal mind has respect for 'supernatural' signs and symbols. I'd like to see some joker's face after he gets one of these darts in him and wakes up to find a silver talon in his hide. It will scare the pants off him."

Paul contributed a few items of his own to the Space Eagle's "bag of tricks," as Julie referred to his equipment. "Do you remember the instant 'plastic surgery' technique developed by the House of Girard after the Viet Nam war?" he asked his sister.

"Of course. The board of directors decided it was too dangerous to release for general medical use."

"Exactly, but wouldn't it be perfect for certain purposes of the Space Eagle?"

Julie's eyes opened wide. "For disguising yourself!" she exclaimed. "Big brother, you're a genius!"

The Girard method of instant "plastic surgery" was the result of intensive research by a team of medical and cosmetic technicians. Stated briefly and in layman's language, the treatment consisted of swallowing a special pill which released a series of powerful hormones and glandular extracts into the subject's bloodstream. Then an ointment was applied externally to the subject's face, head, arms, back, or to whatever portion of the body required the "surgery." The ointment contained a mixture of tiny magnetic isotopes derived from the identical strains of hormones injected into the bloodstream. The magnetic isotopes had the effect of drawing out the hormone serum through the walls of the veins and capillaries, through muscle, flesh, and bone tissue, and finally through the skin and into the ointment itself.

For a period of one hour after this osmosis took place, the muscles, flesh, and bones so affected could be molded and reshaped much as a sculptor shapes a clay figure. After an hour this "meddulafying phenomenon," as it was known technically, began to wear off, and within thirty minutes more the bones, flesh, and muscles of the subject became rigid once again.

Hundreds of horribly disfigured veterans of the Viet Nam war had not been able to believe their eyes when they had looked at themselves in the mirror after being treated by the skilled team of surgeons and cosmeticians from the House of Girard. A man's physical appearance could be so completely altered in just one hour's time that his own family could not recognize him.

The researchers had developed other drugs along similar lines, but they had not been widely used in the operations performed on the disfigured veterans. There was a hormone that could change the color of the skin to any desired tone from jet black to albino white. There was another glandular extract —still in the experimental stage when the project was shelved—that could cause the human body to burn off calories at an enormous rate in a short time. Within a few hours a person who was one hundred pounds overweight could get down to his normal weight.

The next day Paul flew back to Washington for another private audience with the President of the United States. The President was very impressed with the special weapons and equipment with which the Space Eagle would be armed.

To make certain that both the President and Paul could contact each other within seconds in an emergency, a foolproof plan had been worked out by Paul and Julie.

Paul explained it to the President. "The

S.W.I.F.T. will be placed in a permanent orbit around the earth in a dummy shell that will disguise it as just another relay satellite. I can summon it from wherever I am within a few seconds by an electronic signal."

He paused and removed from his ear a small plug that had been invisible to the President until Paul displayed it.

"This little gadget is an electronic marvel. My sister developed it. It's a miniaturized radio transmitter and receiver tuned to a frequency of seven thousand six hundred and sixty kilocycles."

The President laughed. "I like that. Very appropriate. Seventy-six sixty . . . the code numbers of the Space Eagle."

Paul grinned. "Julie's idea. She thought it was cute, among other things." He was always amused by Julie's unexpected show of girlish traits.

"If there is anything else in that frequency now, we'll clear it up," the President promised. "It will be reserved for the Space Eagle."

"Thank you, sir," Paul said quietly. He continued on. "Solar batteries will keep the S.W.I.F.T.'s radio humming twenty-four hours a day. If you want to reach me, Mr. President, all you have to do is to pick up a phone anywhere in the world and dial seventy-six sixty. The signal will be transmitted through the telephone company's main exchange and will be relayed by computer to the S.W.I.F.T.'s receiver. The signal will be relayed back to me wherever I am." He inserted the miniaturized button back into his right ear.

"You are truly an amazing young man, Paul," the President complimented him.

"Thank you, sir," Paul said modestly. "But most of the credit for this has to go to Julie."

"A remarkable girl."

Paul smiled. "Mother would consider it more remarkable of her if she found some nice husband and settled down."

"To be sure." The President laughed. "Mothers are all alike, aren't they?"

A sly smile crept over the President's face. "And now, Paul, there's something I'd like to present to you. Nothing to compare with all those marvelous things Julie gave you, but it's from the heart. From my heart and from the heart of your country, Paul."

He unlocked a drawer of his desk and took out a

leather folder with a handsomely embossed cover. The Presidential Seal was impressed into the leather in silver. He handed it to Paul.

"Open it and read it, son."

Paul flipped open the cover and read the document it contained. It was done in hand lettering in elaborate scroll on heavy parchment.

> By special order of the President of the United States there now exists, as of the date inscribed below, a new department of the United States Government hereafter to be known as the United States Spatial Intelligence Agency.

Paul read on, deeply moved. A lump formed in his throat as his eyes skimmed over the most important section.

> As the first chief of the Spatial Intelligence Agency, the President hereby appoints a man of superior courage, genius, and patriotism. For security reasons this man must remain anonymous, so he can only be referred to in this directive as the Space Eagle. This code name is derived from the silver eagle in the President's Seal and is symbolic of the power and authority. . . .

When he had finished reading, Paul shut the folder and smiled humbly. "All I can say, sir, is thank you. It's a rare honor."

"This document will undoubtedly be enshrined someday in a glass case in the National Museum," the President said. "I haven't signed it formally as yet. I wanted to wait until you got here so I could do so in your presence."

He sat down at his desk and opened the folder. Picking up a pen from a desk set, he wrote his signature at the bottom of the page with a proud flourish. To make it official, he stamped it with the Presidential Seal, a smaller version of the symbol on the leather cover.

"From now on it will be in your keeping, Paul," he said.

"I'll take good care of it, sir. I'll put it in the Top Security Three vault back at the Foundation, safe from prying eyes."

"Good man."

Paul cleared his throat. "Mr. President, I'd like to ask a favor of you."

"Anything, Paul. You name it, and I'll see that you get it."

"I feel guilty asking this, sir. But could I have the pen you signed it with? It would be a priceless memento for my grandchildren."

The President handed over the pen in silence. Both men were too emotionally touched to speak. They shook hands silently.

7.

A MESSAGE
IN BLOOD

Seven weeks passed without any further word from the President. Paul was becoming discouraged. The S.W.I.F.T. was in its orbit, humming smoothly around the earth, its radio silent. Paul tried to work off his impatience by focusing all of his attention on the business of the Foundation and the House of Girard.

One night near the end of November Julie and Paul had supper together.

"You look tired, Paul," she told him with concern. "Why don't you take a vacation?"

"I can't take the time," he said grumpily.

"Oh, come on, now! You've done six months' work in the past seven weeks. If you don't let up, you'll get sick, Paul. I'm serious. Please, Mother

94

and I are both worried about you." She hesitated. "I know what's bothering you. It's your new job with the Spatial Intelligence Agency."

Paul grunted wryly. "That's the trouble. It isn't a job. I have nothing to do."

Her clear, honest, hazel eyes held his. "It just seems that way. After all, the idea is so new and so specialized. I'm sure that cases which come under the jurisdiction of the SIA are very rare, Paul. The President will want to be very sure of what he's doing before he calls in the Space Eagle."

"I suppose you're right," he admitted. He patted her hand. "Maybe you're right about that vacation, too. I think I'll fly over to Switzerland and get in some skiing before the Christmas holidays."

"That's a wonderful idea," Julie said happily. "I only wish I could join you."

The next day Paul left for the famous St. Moritz winter resort in the Swiss Alps. At least a dozen young men and women greeted him as he crossed the lobby upon his arrival at the big inn. They were all jet-set regulars, attractive, gay, charming. Julie thought they were a silly, empty-headed bunch and that Paul was wasting his time on them. The "pretty people" she called them, and not in a complimentary way. Paul secretly agreed with her that they were too rich and irresponsible, but he enjoyed their company on the ski slopes, at the car and air races, and at the other sporting events that he loved so well. Now he turned down a chorus of invitations to come to parties, saying that he wanted to get in some exercise before supper.

A pretty girl with long blond hair and dressed in ski pants and sweater took his arm.

"Paul, dear," she said, "you don't mean you're going on the slopes now. Why, it's snowing, and it will soon be dark."

"She's right, Paul," a husky young man with a foreign accent agreed. "The danger flags have been posted on all the slopes since noon."

Paul smiled at him. "Thank you for warning me, Hans. But that's where the fun is, right? Where the danger is."

The young man clapped Paul on the back and shook his head. "I should have known you'd say that."

The crowd stared after him admiringly as he went across to the elevator.

It was late afternoon when Paul Girard left the inn with his skis slung over one shoulder. Outside, he pulled the hood of his parka tighter about his head and pulled down his goggles. The snow was as fine as sand, and a strong wind whipped it stingingly into his face as he went directly to the expert's run. Alone on the steep hill, he adjusted his boots comfortably in the foot harnesses and pushed off the summit with his ski poles.

In a matter of minutes he was traveling over sixty miles an hour. It was wild and exciting to plunge down the white slope with the icy wind whistling around him and the snow blasting at him from all directions. He thought how funny it was that he should feel more of a thrill moving at sixty miles an hour in such primitive surroundings than he had felt speeding at 1,500,000 miles an hour in outer space.

Next time, though, it would be different, he vowed. What bigger thrill in the world could there be than outracing light itself, moving faster than 186,282 miles per second? He would do it. The S.W.I.F.T. would do it and solve the many mysteries that made up its name: Space Warp Infinity

Finity Transport. One day in the near future, Paul Girard would break the space-time barrier!

At first, he was not aware of the buzzing in his right ear. He thought it must be the wind. But why only in one ear? Then it came to him with a jolt. It was the hidden button radio in his ear signaling to him! He had been waiting for this moment for seven weeks, and now that it had arrived, he had almost ignored it!

He cut off the ski run into a grove of pines where he knew there was a rough log refuge shack for weary skiers to rest. He skidded to a stop in front of the door, kicked off his skis, and went inside, out of the fierce fury of the storm.

He quickly removed the radio from his ear and cupped it in the palm of one hand. "Space Eagle here . . . seventy-six sixty," he barked into the dual mike and speaker.

He recognized the President's voice at once, faint but clear. The Chief Executive sounded tense and agitated.

"We finally have something for your department —something very big, by the looks of things. One of our CIA agents was found dead in Hong Kong

last night. A Chinese chap. He's the fourth Intelligence casualty in that vicinity in less than one week."

Paul whistled in surprise. "That does sound big, sir."

"This last man," the President continued, "had a hollow pivot tooth designed for hiding microfilm. Whoever murdered him got everything else he had on his body, but they missed the tooth. Inside the tooth was a small scrap of rice paper with a simple message scratched on it in blood—probably with a pin."

"What was the message?" Paul asked tersely.

"It read: 'On December twenty-fifth, Muta will wipe out the United States . . . maybe the world!' "

"That's all?" Paul exclaimed.

"That's all."

"Whatever does it mean? And who is Muta?"

"The CIA believes it refers to Dr. Lachesis Muta. Until he disappeared some years back, Lachesis Muta was considered to be one of the most brilliant scientific minds in the West."

"He was on our team, then?"

"We thought so then. His ancestry is a mixture

of Chinese, Tibetan, Russian, and Syrian, but he was a naturalized American. He worked at Oak Ridge on top-security projects in the forties and fifties. From 1960 through 1966 he taught nuclear physics and space math at the University of California. The next year he went to Tokyo University for a year on an international teacher exchange program. A short while after he and his family had settled in Tokyo, he kissed his wife and children good-bye one night and went out for a stroll. He never returned. There were rumors that he was kidnapped or had defected to the Chinese Reds, but Peking denied both stories. There was no proof. He's never been heard from again. It's as though Lachesis Muta just vanished from the face of the earth."

"Until that message in blood," Paul said soberly. "You're sure the 'Muta' in the message and the missing professor are the same man?"

"We can't be sure of anything. That's why I called in the Space Eagle. We can't afford to sacrifice any more conventional agents in suicide missions behind the Bamboo Curtain. This is a job for the Space Eagle, with his special advantages."

"I agree, sir," Paul said with a swell of pride. At

last his star was going to rise. "You think Lachesis Muta is somewhere in China, then?"

"As I said, Washington is in the dark. For all we know the message could be just another piece of wild Communist propaganda to give the United States a case of the jitters. But we can't afford to ignore it. Suppose the Reds truly are cooking up some fiendish plot against us. Anyway, it will be your job to check this thing out and track it back to its origin. If you need any help, the whole United States Intelligence system has been alerted to give you anything you want."

"Thank you, sir. I'll do my best." Paul was sober, but he was tingling with excitement from the tips of his fingers to the tips of his toes.

"Good luck, Space Eagle," the President said before he hung up the phone.

Paul sat in the cold shack with the wind screaming around the roof and hammering on the windows, running the story the President had told him over and over in his mind like a film. The President had said the message might be a crackpot Communist lie. That was possible. Yet four men had been killed, four United States Intelligence agents, in the Orient in less than a week. That could mean that these agents had gotten on to something very, very big. Something as big as the destruction of the United States? Paul wondered. How could one man —Lachesis Muta, if it were he—accomplish such a fantastic thing? The first thing to do was to get some background on Muta.

Paul removed a small address book from his shirt pocket and opened it. It looked like an ordinary little black book, such as any young man might carry, containing the names and phone numbers of a string of young women. Actually, the listings were the coded names and numbers of the various government agencies in the capital.

Paul found the phone number for the director of the Central Intelligence Agency. Then he unscrewed one half of the tiny button transmitter-receiver, revealing a microscopic dial, exactly like the dials on regulation telephones. From a pocket of his parka he took out a jeweler's eyepiece of the type used by watchmakers to magnify the inner workings of a clock. Fitting the eyepiece to one eye, he squinted at the dial and, with a straight pin, dialed his number.

Far across the Atlantic Ocean, a group of four men were sprawled out in chairs in the office of the director of the Central Intelligence Agency, listening to a briefing with grinning faces.

"All I can tell you is what the directive says," the director said gruffly. His face was red. "We don't argue with Presidential directives. If the chief says this character gets top priority no matter what he asks for, then he gets top priority."

His assistant, a beefy, balding man, laughed. "Come on, Al. This has to be some kind of joke. The Space Eagle! He just can't be for real."

"That must be it," another man agreed. "Somebody is playing a joke on us. Maybe the Pentagon? Or how about the FBI? They've been itching to get even with us for winning the bowling championship this year."

In the midst of the talking and laughing the director's private telephone began to ring. Only three men outside of the President had this private number as far as the director knew. He silenced the other men and picked up the phone.

"Yes?" he said sharply. His mouth flew open in surprise as a rich, deep voice crackled in the earpiece of his phone with the words, *"Space Eagle here . . . seventy-six sixty."*

The director looked around at the puzzled faces in his office, stunned. "It's no joke," he told them. "He's on my line right now. The Space Eagle!"

The CIA gave Paul a thorough rundown on the background of Dr. Lachesis Muta. From their report he picked out what he hoped would prove to be a good lead. The missing professor had a grown son, a university instructor, who was living in San Francisco. His name was Addison Muta. Lachesis Muta's former friends and colleagues had told the FBI and the CIA at the time of his disappearance that the doctor had loved this son very much. Addison had been his favorite child. Furthermore, the rest of the Muta family were now living with relatives in Syria.

Paul reasoned that if it was true that Lachesis Muta had discovered some fiendish power with which he could destroy the United States, he would not do the terrible deed *so long as his beloved son, Addison, was living in the target area.*

"Are you sure that Addison Muta is still in San Francisco?" he asked the CIA director.

"Yes," the reply came back. "As a matter of fact, I got a report about him this morning from the FBI boys on the West Coast. As soon as we learned of that strange message that was found on our dead agent in Hong Kong, we asked the FBI to check into Muta's son. According to the report, he's a solid citizen. He's well liked by the students and his fellow teachers at the university. He's not tied in with the Reds. We're sure of that."

He paused. "There's just one thing. The janitor in the apartment house where he lives said that for the past week young Muta has been receiving regular midnight visits from three men. Some of the neighbors had complained about the loud talking in his apartment, as if they were arguing."

"Did anyone ever see these men?" Paul asked tensely.

"Yes, seems they were orientals."

An electric chill coursed through Paul's body. His voice was anxious. "Get in touch with the FBI in San Francisco at once. Tell them to keep a watch on Addison Muta around the clock. Under no conditions are they to allow him to leave the city, even if they have to take him into protective custody."

"Protective custody?" the director exclaimed. "On what charge?"

"Let the FBI figure that out for themselves." Paul's voice hardened. "That's an order, sir. You can check it out with the President if you care to."

"That won't be necessary," the director said respectfully. "We already have our orders from the President. The Space Eagle has top priority. Only the President himself can countermand your orders."

"Thank you," Paul said, his voice soft and polite now. "You can tell the FBI that I will be in San Francisco by tomorrow night and that I will contact them personally."

"Yes, sir, Space Eagle. I'll tell them."

Paul signed off, put the button radio back together, and slipped it into his ear. He buttoned his parka, pulled down his goggles, and rushed out into the snowstorm. Every minute was precious. The date was December 4. The message had said that Muta would strike on December 25. If the mad doctor was not bluffing, it meant that the Space Eagle had only three weeks to foil the diabolical scheme. He felt as if he were sitting on a time bomb, with each tick of the clock bringing the United

States and maybe the world closer to death and disaster!

The more he thought about it, the more angry and indignant Paul grew. His fingers itched to get hold of Lachesis Muta. Only a low snake could plot such horror for what should have been a very merry Christmas day!

8.

TRANSFORMATION

THE FOLLOWING morning Paul walked into Julie's office at the Girard Foundation. The girl blinked in surprise.

"Back so soon?" she joked. "What happened? Wouldn't the playgirls and playboys let you into their games?"

"No joking matter, sister," Paul said gravely. He told her about the emergency call from the President. "So I'm on my way to San Francisco," he finished up. "As far as everyone at the Foundation and the House of Girard knows, this will be just another routine business trip. I'll actually check in at our West Coast plant to make it look good."

"Do be careful, Paul," Julie said anxiously.

He smiled. "Don't you worry about me, little

sister. I can take care of myself. Before I leave, though, I'd like to pick up the talon gun and the disguise kit."

Julie took him down to the Top Security Three lab and opened the vault. "I've worked up another little item for the Space Eagle," she said with a note of pride.

"Oh?" He was puzzled when she turned to him with a pair of men's brown shoes in her hands. "Julie, what on earth?"

She wrinkled up her nose in an impish grin. "Don't worry; they're the right size."

"But *shoes!*" he protested. "I have a closetful of shoes."

"Not shoes like these," she said mysteriously. She turned one over and ran her hand across the leather sole. To Paul's astonishment, the whole bottom of the shoe came open like a swinging door. Inside the secret compartment was a small, flat talon gun and a supply of the tranquilizer darts.

"Very clever," he said with a smile.

She repeated the process with the other shoe. In its hidden compartment were the pills and ointments required for him to transform his appearance.

110

Paul put one arm fondly around his sister's shoulders. "Julie, what *would* I do without you?"

"Thank you," she said sweetly. "I just don't want to see the Space Eagle get his wings clipped."

That night Paul checked in at a fashionable San Francisco hotel and promptly telephoned the local office of the FBI. They told him that Addison Muta was under surveillance around the clock as he had ordered. Nothing unusual had happened since the last report. Paul thanked them and hung up.

He went into the bathroom and lined up his pills and ointments on the shelf under the shaving mirror. He swallowed one of the hormone pills, then smeared the cream containing magnetic isotopes on his face and neck and waited for the medullafying, or softening, effect to take place.

Paul Girard was a talented amateur sculptor. One of his works, the bust of a former American President, was on display in the National Museum in Washington, D.C. Now, as he felt the bones and tissues of his face and neck turn into jelly, his skilled fingers went to work. At first it gave him a strange sensation to watch his hands mold and reshape his own flesh and bone as if they were clay. There was no pain, no feeling at all in his face. It was something like getting a shot of novocaine at the dentist's office.

Paul pushed his nose this way and that with the heel of his hand until he had the desired shape. Then he put the forefinger of each hand in a corner of his mouth and pulled, stretching his lips. He had no particular model in mind as he worked. He formed a rather large, square, pleasant face with a wide, upturned nose. Satisfied, he went back into the bedroom to lie down and wait for the chemicals to wear off. About one hour later his new face had set. Bones, flesh, and muscles were firm and normal. He looked into the mirror and smiled with satisfaction. If he were to meet Julie and his mother on the street they would pass him by without a flicker of recognition.

Leaving the hotel, he got into a taxicab and gave the driver Addison Muta's address.

Paul introduced himself to Addison Muta as a magazine writer doing an article on Lachesis Muta, Addison's father. At first Addison refused to let Paul into his apartment.

A slim young man of about twenty-five, Addison was as tall as Paul but much lighter. He had straight black hair and enormous dark eyes. His skin was sallow, and he had a sharp nose like the beak of a hawk.

"I'm sorry, but I can't help you," Addison said. "I haven't heard from my father since I was a boy. Anyway, I'm not interested in talking about him."

"Please, Mr. Muta," Paul pleaded. "At least let me tell my editor that I talked to you. He's liable to fire me if I come back empty-handed."

Young Muta was a softhearted man, and he finally let Paul come inside. "But make it fast," he warned. "I have an early class at the university."

Paul learned nothing from Addison that he didn't already know, but that he had expected. His purpose in talking to the missing professor's son was to cover up his true reason for visiting the apartment.

The large, gaudy tie clip Paul wore was a small candid camera. While they spoke, he secretly snapped pictures of Addison from different angles. As he scribbled notes in a pad on the low coffee table in front of the living room couch, Paul slyly slipped his left hand under the table and stuck a tiny electronic listening device on the underside, where it would be invisible unless the table was turned over. It was a typical "bugging" transmitter of the kind used by private detectives and law enforcement agencies, only it was supersensitive. Specially designed by Julie Girard, it would transmit—to a range of twenty-five miles—on the 7660-kilocycle frequency to the button receiver inside Paul's ear.

Once the "bug" was in place and he had his photographs, Paul cut the interview short. "Thanks for your help, Mr. Muta," he said. "At least I can tell the boss I saw you."

The young man was apologetic. "I wish I could have told you more about my father," he said. "It's just that I don't know anything about where he is or what he's doing."

"Then you do know he's alive at least?" Paul asked.

Addison Muta's pale face reddened slightly. "I don't know for sure, of course, but it is my belief that he is alive."

Paul looked him squarely in the eyes. Addison turned away. It was obvious that he did know something about Lachesis Muta that he wasn't saying.

Paul didn't push it, however. He shook hands with the man and left.

Back at his hotel, Paul sat down in front of the television set and watched an old science fiction movie on the late show. It was all very silly stuff, he thought, but it served to keep him awake during his vigil.

The movie was half over when Paul's ear radio buzzed into action. Addison Muta had late visitors, and from the sound of their voices they were Chinese. Paul, a brilliant student of the modern languages at Oxford, immediately placed the dialect. They came from the vicinity of Peking.

Addison was apparently very angry. "This is the last time you are to come here. If you won't let me alone, I'll put this matter in the hands of the police."

An oily, hissing voice answered him. "Don't be foolish, my boy. What charges would you file against us? We are merely old friends of your father who have come to see you on a mission of mercy. Lachesis Muta is old and sick. He wants to see his favorite son before he dies. Is there any crime to that?"

"I don't believe he's dying," Addison said dryly.

"It's a trick to get me to come with you, that's all. Why he would want to see me after all these years, I don't know."

"He loves you—his son."

Addison laughed. "Why did he leave me, then? He abandoned the whole family."

Paul heard the Chinese speaker sigh. "There are duties that come before personal feelings. He had no choice."

"What is all this mystery about?" Addison demanded angrily. "You won't even tell me where my father is."

"A matter of security. You will find out soon enough."

"I won't go!" Addison said firmly. "If my father wants to see me, let him come here!"

The hissing of a chorus of angry oriental voices buzzed in Paul's ear.

"You *must* come with us," a deeper voice said. "If you remain here, your life is in danger."

"Are you threatening me?" Addison demanded.

"Not in the least. We are trying to save your life. Your father has sent us here to save you."

"That's the most insane thing I ever heard of!"

young Muta shouted. "Now, get out! And stay out!"

Finally they left. Paul could hear Addison stomping around his apartment, grumbling to himself. "Bunch of loonies," he muttered. "Silly story. My life is in danger. From what? Nonsense!" He began to laugh.

In the hotel, Paul Girard was not laughing. Nonsense? He didn't think so. Paul was sure, now, that Dr. Lachesis Muta was deadly serious about his business. He was going to destroy the United States— or, at any rate, try his best to do so. The mad doctor was apparently very confident, too, that his foul plan would succeed. Otherwise, why would he send a delegation halfway around the world to beg his favorite son to leave the country?

The early morning air blew in through the open window and raised goose bumps on Paul's bare arms. Or was it the cold that made him shiver? he wondered. The date was December 6! There were only nineteen days left to him—nineteen days to find Lachesis Muta, to learn what he was up to, and to stop his design for mass murder. Was it possible? Paul didn't know. But he would do his level best.

His body and mind were begging for rest, but Paul knew he could not sleep yet. There was too much to be done and too little time in which to do it.

He phoned the FBI office. "Space Eagle here . . . seventy-six sixty," he snapped.

"Yes, *sir!*" the regional bureau director answered.

"I want you to pick up Addison Muta as soon as possible," Paul directed the man. "I want him held in protective custody indefinitely. And in the utmost secrecy."

"But, sir," the regional director protested, "we can't arrest a private citizen without a reason. What are we protecting him from?"

"I don't know yet, but I intend to find out. You have your orders, chief. See that they are carried out to the letter. This request is a Space Eagle Top Priority one. If you care to check with—"

"Yes, I know," the man interrupted. "I can check with the President. No need to do that, sir. We'll pick up young Muta right away."

"Good. Once he's safely put away, just sit tight until you hear from me again." Paul hung up.

Next he went into the bathroom, turned out the

light, and developed the roll of film he had shot with the tie-clip camera in Muta's apartment. While the negatives were drying, he set up his enlarger, which Julie had invented for the Army Signal Corps. It was a pair of field glasses that could be broken down and converted in about three minutes for photo reconnaissance work in the field.

In less than a half hour he had six big prints spread out on the dresser in his room. They were clear and sharp and showed Addison Muta full-face, in profile, and from a three-quarter angle. Then he got out his disguise kit again and went to work.

When he was done, the first light of dawn was seeping through the room's venetian blinds. He looked at his reflection in the mirror and was amazed at the total effect. Addison Muta's twin brother was staring back at him out of the glass!

There was a final task. Paul was about forty pounds heavier than the doctor's son. He made some calculations on a slip of paper to determine the exact amount of tissue-shrinking hormone he would have to inject into his body. Then, after giving himself the dose, he lay down on the bed to catch a few hours' sleep.

When he awoke, the sun was streaming into the room. He looked at his arms. They seemed to be as thin as pipestems. His rock-hard, athletic muscles had withered. Walking into the bathroom, he got on the scale. It showed a reading just thirty-eight pounds below his normal weight. His body had burned off the excess calories while he was asleep. Now he was ready for the dangerous, perhaps impossible, task that lay ahead.

When he reached Addison Muta's apartment house, he went down an alley and slipped into the service entrance. Climbing a back stairway, he reached the third floor and hurried down the hall to Muta's apartment. He tried three skeleton keys before he found the right one. The door swung in, and Paul walked into the empty parlor.

He took off his own baggy clothes and dressed in Muta's clothing. For the rest of the day, he stood before the mirror in the bedroom talking to himself and making faces in the glass. In his college days, Paul had been a superb actor and mimic. In his senior year, a talent scout for a major movie studio had seen him perform in a college theatrical production and tried to sign him to a contract, but

121

Paul had politely turned it down.

His acting was a bit rusty after all these years, but it soon came back to him. By late afternoon he was making real headway. His imitation of Addison Muta's voice, manner, and way of walking was so good that he almost began to believe that he was young Muta.

"I suppose that's what they mean by method acting," he mused to himself.

Finally he decided he was ready to face the world. There was nothing more he could do now except wait. From here on it was up to the other side. He prayed they would not hesitate too long. Another day was almost gone, another precious twenty-four hours would soon tick by. The clock on the mantel of the parlor's imitation fireplace ticked off the seconds terrifyingly fast!

9.

"PRINCE OF DARKNESS"

Paul marked time for the next three days. He did nothing except sit around Addison Muta's apartment, eating, sleeping, and watching television. Every evening he went for a long walk that took him through the Chinese section of the city and along the dark and lonely waterfront. These walks were the most important part of his plan. If he had guessed right, Lachesis Muta's oriental henchmen had orders not to leave San Francisco and the United States without young Addison. Since Addison had refused to go along with them voluntarily, there was only one way open to them. They would have to kidnap him!

If Paul had guessed wrong, however, the Chinese might have given up on Addison. They might already be on their way back to China or wherever they had come from. That would mean that he, the Space Eagle, was wasting precious time doing nothing while the world edged closer and closer to the brink of disaster. He would have to take the chance. There was no other way to find Dr. Lachesis Muta and find out what he was up to.

On the night of December 10 he bundled up in one of Addison's overcoats and mufflers and went out to take his evening stroll. A cold wind was whipping icy rain across the bay. The droplets stung his face and froze in his hair. The dark waterfront streets were even more deserted than they usually were. A few seamen passed him with their coat collars turned up and their hands jammed into the pockets of their pea coats. The mournful sound of a foghorn rolled across the water.

Paul shivered and turned into a narrow, lampless street. He could see scarcely ten feet ahead of him. As he passed a shadowy alleyway, he saw black, catlike shapes moving toward him. Strong hands pinned his arms behind him, and a cloth saturated with chloroform was slapped over his face. He put up a feeble struggle to make it look good, but his muscles turned to jelly as the strong anesthetic took effect. The street began to spin like a pinwheel. Then everything faded into blackness.

Paul regained consciousness slowly. His head ached, and there was a strange, rhythmic throbbing in his ears. He was lying in a small room on a wall bunk. He opened his eyes and stared at the wall alongside the bunk. It was metal plating. He knew, then, where he was—in a cabin aboard a ship. The throbbing in his ears was the ship's engines. He got to his feet and walked to a porthole on the far wall. It was daylight, cold and gray. The choppy Pacific Ocean stretched away into the wintery mists.

At the sound of a lock grating he whirled around. The door swung open, and two Chinese men stepped into the room. One of them, a stout man with a small chin beard, smiled pleasantly at Paul.

"Ah, so. You are awake at last. Please accept our humblest apologies for any pain and inconvenience we have caused you. But it was necessary. Soon you will see that, and you will forgive us."

"I doubt that very much," Paul said, his voice carefully pitched to sound like Addison Muta's. "What is the meaning of this, gentlemen?"

125

The stout man bowed his head. "Your father will explain all to you when you see him."

Paul's heart leaped with excitement. He had guessed right! They were taking him to the hiding place of Dr. Lachesis Muta!

"I have no wish to see my father," he said coldly. "I demand that you return me to San Francisco at once."

The two Chinese looked at each other sorrowfully. "That is quite impossible, Mr. Muta. Within ten minutes a plane will be catapulted from the deck of this freighter. You will be aboard it. Within six hours you will land at your destination."

Paul pretended to be indignant. "I must warn you that kidnapping is a federal crime, gentlemen. At the first opportunity I will report you to the authorities."

The skinny Chinese covered his mouth with a hand and began to giggle.

Paul was taken out on deck to the forward hatch. From deep inside the ship a hydraulic elevator lifted a small jet transport plane topside. It was a sleek little craft. Printed on its side in silver lettering were the words: PACIFIC COAST AIRWAYS. He recognized the name as a reputable airline with which the House of Girard had often done business.

The pilot and copilot climbed aboard, followed by Paul and his two escorts. The elevator tilted so that the plane's pointed nose was aimed at the sky at an angle of about forty-five degrees.

"We'll be launched by jet catapult," the bearded Chinese informed Paul. "Fasten your seat belt, please."

There were two sharp blasts. The ship trembled, then shot into the air like an arrow from a bow. Her twin jet engines burped into life. Then she lost momentum and seemed to hang motionless in the air for a moment until the jet exhausts belched fire. Paul was pressed back against his seat as the streamlined rocket plane climbed faster and faster into the mesosphere. It leveled off at fifty miles up and set its course to the east.

Paul shut his eyes and slouched in his seat. It was a good time to catch up on his sleep. From the looks of things, he was going to need all the strength and energy he could muster. In his dreams he saw the page of a calendar. The date was in big red letters which were dripping blood. It was December 25!

Hours later, the excited voices of the four Chinese in the plane woke him up. The jet transport had descended into the atmosphere once more and was cruising at a speed which he estimated to be about five hundred miles per hour. Squinting out of a round port, he saw the sea rolling below. Up ahead he could make out the coastline dimly. He thought it must be the China coast. Minutes later, he knew he was right when a swarm of military jet rocket planes appeared on the horizon. As they drew closer, he recognized the insignia of the Red China Air Force painted on their fuselages.

The stout Chinese with the beard smiled at Paul. "Here comes our escort," he said. "This is quite an honor for you, Mr. Muta. You will understand now what a man of importance your illustrious father is in the East."

"Yes," Paul said with a dry mouth. Lachesis Muta was going to be a dangerous foe, of that there was no doubt. He only hoped the Space Eagle would be a match for Muta and his evil designs.

From the moment they crossed the China coast, Paul was on the alert. He studied every mile of the terrain over which they flew, tracing their course on a vivid map of China in his mind. They were traveling southwest, in the general direction of India. The land below grew more rocky and wild. Snow covered the ground. The mountains became more jagged and towered higher into the sky. He had a pretty good idea of where they were headed now—Tibet.

The rocket plane began to circle one high peak topped by a flat mesa, or plateau. To Paul it looked no different than any of the surrounding terrain. It was covered with snow and ice unmarked by any footprints or other signs that man or beast had been there. The plane slowed and began to descend.

"Fasten your seat belt," the stout Chinese ordered. "We're going to make a vertical landing."

The pilot brought up the nose of the ship until it was hovering over the center of the plateau at a full ninety-degree angle with the ground below. It seemed to hang motionless in the air, held aloft by the gentle thrust of retro-rockets and balanced by its gyroscopes. Skillfully the pilot cut down the rocket engines, and the ship descended to the smooth surface of the plateau. There was a soft bump as it settled down in the snow.

Paul looked out the port at his side and exclaimed, "You mean to say my father lives here?"

The bearded Chinese chuckled. "Patience, young man. Patience."

Suddenly Paul had the sensation that the plane was sinking deeper into the snow. It seemed to be rising on all sides of them in huge drifts. The port windows were blacked out as it covered them. Abruptly he realized what was happening. The section of the plateau where the ship had landed was a large turntable. They were descending into an elevator shaft that went down deep into the interior of the mountain.

Finally the elevator turntable shuddered to a stop. Paul looked out the window and saw a crew of men in black coveralls swarming around the plane. He heard the rumble of a winch motor. Slowly the nose of the ship was lowered until they were on a horizontal plane again.

The Chinese beside him smiled and unbuckled his seat belt. "We have arrived, Mr. Muta. You have entered the domain of the Magnificent Muta, your eminent parent. I know he is waiting anxiously to greet you."

130

They disembarked from the plane and walked down a long, well-lighted corridor.

Paul's stout Chinese escort explained it to him. "This mountain is like a huge beehive. There are twenty levels like this one. On each level the corridors run out from the center like the spokes of a wheel."

They reached the end of the corridor and were admitted to the central chamber by armed, uniformed guards. The central chamber was an immense circular vault whose walls were covered with electronic equipment—flashing lights, dials and gauges, switches, neon tubes. All of the equipment was clicking and buzzing away busily under the watchful eyes of technicians in white coveralls. Most of the faces, Paul saw, were oriental, but there were some Caucasians and Negroes among them, too.

In the center of the chamber was an open well protected by a circular metal railing. Paul and his guide walked over to the railing. Pipes, ducts, and heavy cables ran down through this open well from one level to the other. Paul leaned over the railing and peered down. He counted ten levels plunging into the depths of the mountain. He strained his eyes upward and saw that they were an equal distance from the top of the "beehive," as the Chinese had called it.

"This is the control and administration center," the man answered his unspoken question. "Come, we must not keep your father waiting. You will have ample time to learn about all these wonders of his later."

Wonders, indeed! Paul thought uneasily. Even from the little he had seen of this fantastic underground world, he had to admit that the man who had created it must be a genius. Lachesis Muta had built a city, a fortress, inside a snow-capped mountain peak on the very roof of the world. It was an engineering miracle. Paul no longer had any doubt about the powers of this mad genius. If Muta said he could destroy the United States, he probably had the means and the will to do just that. The big question was, could he be stopped?

Taking a deep breath, Paul turned to his companion. "Yes, let us go to my father."

They left the big chamber and walked to the end of another corridor. At the end of the corridor was a heavy, polished steel door. In the center of the

132

door was a blank television screen. The Chinese guide stood directly in front of the screen and spoke into a small microphone beneath it.

"The mission has been successfully carried out, Master," he said proudly. "Your son is here."

Slowly the steel door slid open. Behind it was an elegant office with thick carpeting, soft, diffused lighting, and expensive furnishings. It reminded Paul of his own office at the House of Girard's executive offices in New York. Opposite the door was an enormous desk. And seated behind the desk was a man who could be, Paul knew, none other than Dr. Lachesis Muta himself.

As they entered, he sprang up and rushed around the desk. He was tall and thin, almost gaunt, with a long, hollow face and deep-set eyes that burned with the fires of genius and madness. His hair and small, pointed beard were streaked with gray. He was dressed in the oriental fashion, wearing a loose tunic and black trousers made of a shapeless, silken material.

"Welcome, my son," he said in a voice that had the rich quality of a deep organ tone. "What a wonderful moment this is for me, seeing you again."

He held out his arms as he advanced across the room, but Paul's cold and distant manner and expression stopped him. Studying the younger man's face with his keen, bright eyes, Muta frowned.

"What is it, Addison? Is something wrong?"

Paul laughed harshly. "You certainly didn't expect me to cry for joy, Father, after all these years. Not after the way you walked out and left us alone without a word in Tokyo."

"Yes, I understand." Muta's shoulders slumped. "You must be very bitter, my son, and I don't blame you. But you must believe that what I did caused me more sorrow than it gave to you, my loved ones. I've never stopped loving you—especially you, Addison. You know you were always my favorite." He held out a hand toward Paul once more.

Paul refused to take the hand. "Please, Father," he said. "There are some things that one cannot forgive so easily."

Muta's haggard face brightened. "That is true, my son. But you will forgive me in time. I will make you understand everything. I swear it." He nodded curtly at the guide. "You may go, now, Chan. I want to be alone with my son."

The little bearded man bowed from the waist. "Yes, Master." He backed out of the room hastily, and the steel door slid closed with a hissing sound.

Paul went directly to the point. "All right, Father, why did you have me kidnapped from my home in San Francisco and brought over here to this terrible place in the middle of nowhere?"

"I wanted my son near me."

Paul laughed. "That's a lie! You haven't thought about me for years."

"That is not true." Muta's voice was sincerely hurt. "No day ever went by that I didn't think of you."

"Then why did you leave us?"

Muta sighed. "There are duties men have that must come before their personal desires, even before love. Every good soldier knows that."

"What kind of duties?" Paul asked, his heart beating faster.

"Our first duty is to mankind and to the future of civilization," Muta said. His great, booming voice grew louder and louder as he talked. His face twitched. His eyes seemed to throw off sparks.

"This world, civilization as we know it in the

twentieth century, is doomed. Millions of people killed in world wars. Millions more killed in smaller wars. Russia and the United States threatening each other and smaller nations with the nuclear bomb. The United Nations has been trying for years to straighten out the world without success. It failed. Everything has failed. Civilization is dying a slow and painful death. If things go on the way they've been going, in another century the earth will be a dead, empty planet. All desert and skeletons. The vultures will be all that is left."

Paul was puzzled. "And it's your idea that you can save the world?"

"I *know* I can save it," Muta said, his eyes blazing.

"How?"

"By destroying the diseased part of it, in the same way a physician cuts out the diseased portion of the human body when it is dying from a dread disease. I am going to destroy three-quarters of this world, this civilization, this culture. It is the only answer. In the wake of annihilation, there will be nothing. No law, no order, nothing but raw material. The survivors will be frightened sheep looking for someone, some new power, to help them and guide them.

I, Lachesis Muta, will lead them out of the wilderness into a new life, a new world. We will begin again as Noah did in the old days after the great flood." Muta threw his long, bony arms high into the air and laughed with a hysteria that sent cold chills along Paul's spine.

"I will be king, Addison!" he ranted. "And you, my son, will be my prince!"

Prince of darkness! Paul thought grimly.

10.

A DIABOLICAL
PLAN

IN JUST TWO weeks," Lachesis Muta said, "the
United States will be a smoking hole in the earth,
totally destroyed. That is why I had to bring you
here, Addison. I could not bear to see my beloved
son shrivel up like an ash and die."

"Shrivel up like an ash?" Paul asked.

"Yes, in a nuclear holocaust."

"That's ridiculous, Father. What are you saying?"

Muta smiled fiendishly. "You shall see for yourself, my son." He clapped his hands together once,
smartly. There was the sound of shuffling footsteps.
Paul's attention was drawn to a doorway at one side
of the office. His eyebrows arched in surprise at
what he saw.

A huge figure, at least seven feet tall, filled the

doorway. It had the shape of a man, but there was something about it not quite human. The flesh had a queer waxen look about it. The blue eyes were too vacant. The powerful fingers were like coiled steel springs. It was wearing a pair of black coveralls similar to the dress of the workmen Paul had seen.

"This is Mozzo, my personal bodyguard," Muta introduced the brute. "Mozzo is the most superior robot ever devised by man."

Paul saw it then. The thing was not flesh and blood. What seemed to be flesh and skin was in reality a plastic covering for its metal parts. Still, it was an amazing lifelike creation.

Muta described the robot briefly. "Mozzo's electronic computer brain was programmed with an encephalogram taken of my own brain. Its thought waves are identical to mine. You could say its brain *is* my brain. I don't even have to give verbal commands to it. Up to a distance of one mile it receives my commands in the same way a radio receiver pulls in radio waves. Naturally, it is obedient to no one but me."

"That's amazing," Paul said, and he meant it.

Was there no limit to this man's brilliance? It was a tragedy that such a brain was dedicated to evil instead of good.

"Now we will go down to the missile silos," Muta said.

They left the office and walked down the corridor to an elevator. The elevator took them down to the last level of the underground city. They stepped out onto a floor of rough stone, into a chamber with a domed roof. A balcony ran around the sides of the chamber about ten feet above ground level. Crouching on the balcony were grim-faced guards in black uniforms with jagged streaks of yellow lightning emblazoned across their chests. Their hard, slanted eyes and the muzzles of their strange-looking weapons were trained on the three figures as they emerged from the elevator car.

"Laser rifles," Muta explained with a smile. "They could cut up Mozzo into scrap metal in the blink of an eye, and Mozzo is constructed of the hardest vanadium steel."

"I trust none of them has an itchy trigger finger," Paul observed.

"No fear," Muta assured him. "These guards are

programmed with drugs that make their minds and reflexes almost as efficient and mistake-proof as Mozzo's computer brain. They are my first line of missile security. If anyone other than myself were to get off that elevator, he would be destroyed without question. In fact, if I were to try to enter the missile control room alone, without Mozzo, they would kill me."

Paul's eyebrows lifted in amazement. "I don't understand, Father."

Muta's black eyes glittered. "I have over one thousand technicians and soldiers working here in this fortress. Suppose one of them should be a spy? Suppose such a spy could slip a mind-control drug into my food or drink by which he could compel me to sabotage my grand project. You see, although my human brain pattern could possibly be altered by treachery, Mozzo's computer brain could never be changed. Mozzo's brain is programmed so that it will short-circuit if my electrical brain impulses show any radical, chemically-induced shift. The robot will become immobile, paralyzed you might say, immediately. So, if I try to enter the control room alone, the guards have orders to kill me just as they would kill any impostor or spy."

Paul wiped the perspiration from his forehead with a sleeve. It was diabolical. The mad genius had thought of everything. From the looks of things, it was nearly impossible to stop him from carrying out his plans.

They passed through a bank of steel doors into a second, smaller chamber and a third chamber. Each chamber had been hollowed out of solid rock deep inside the base of the mountain. In each room were two sentries armed with laser rifles. Like the guards on the balcony, they had orders to kill anyone who entered, unless accompanied by Mozzo and Muta *together!*

From the third rock chamber they entered the control center. The four walls of the missile control center were covered with electronic equipment from floor to ceiling. Flashing colored lights blinded Paul. The humming of generators and monitoring devices vibrated his eardrums. A row of thirteen small television screens spread across the front of the main control panel. His eyes scanned the images on the screens with chilling disbelief. There was no mistaking what they were—intercontinental ballistic missiles, ICBM's, with snub-nosed nuclear war-heads! Thirteen of them nestling snugly in their concrete silos, pointing eagerly—almost impatiently, it seemed—at the heavens. Thin streams of wispy vapor curled out of their finned tails. They were ready to go at a moment's notice.

"There they are," Muta said with the pride of a boasting father. "These are the eggs, one could say, from which my perfect new world will be hatched."

Paul could scarcely disguise his horror. He swallowed hard and struggled to keep his voice calm. "I still don't understand," he said. "What can you possibly hope to accomplish with thirteen missiles? Perhaps wipe out a few major cities in the United States, but that's all."

"You think so?" Muta laughed with fiendish delight. "Here, have a look at this, my son." He pushed a button beneath the monitoring screens, and the camera lenses which were trained on the silos zoomed in for close-ups of the missiles.

Paul could not believe his eyes. Stamped on the outer casing of seven of the big ICBM's was the inscription: *U.S.A.* The other six bore the label: *U.S.S.R.*

"I don't understand," he said.

Muta laughed. "The beauty of my plan is that it is so simple, Addison. Precisely at midnight on December twenty-fourth, my thirteen missiles will be launched. They will arc through space to a point above the North Pole. There the gyro autopilots will change their course and send them veering off for their respective targets—the seven marked *U.S.A.* toward the largest cities in Russia, the six marked *U.S.S.R.* toward the largest cities in the United States. When Russian radar picks up the incoming unidentified flying objects, they will think, naturally, that the United States has launched a sneak attack across the Pole. The North American Air Defense Command, likewise, will believe that the Soviet Union is attacking the United States. Within minutes after their big cities have been demolished, the U.S.A. and the U.S.S.R. will be engaged in full-scale nuclear warfare."

Paul's voice was unsteady. "Isn't it possible that both the Russians and the Americans may suspect that the attacks on their cities are a trick by some third party to lure them into a major war?"

Muta rubbed his hands together with pleasure.

"I've taken care of that possibility as well. Two of my thirteen missiles have dummy warheads, so they will crash pretty much intact. If by any small chance the Russians and Americans do delay their retaliatory attacks after the first bombs land on their cities, whatever doubts they have will be removed when the dummy missiles are recovered and examined. The United States will find an ICBM clearly marked *U.S.S.R.* And the Soviet Union will have what seems to be a missile from the arsenal of the U.S.A. The American President and the Russian Premier will push the buttons, have no fear."

Paul held on to the edge of a table to steady himself. It was a terrible nightmare. Try as he would, he could find no fault with the mad doctor's reasoning. For decades the Russians and the Americans had faced each other tensely across half of the world, each watching and waiting for the other to start trouble. They were like two gunfighters in the American Wild West, Paul thought, circling each other suspiciously with their gun hands poised to go for their six-shooters. There was no doubt in his mind at all that Lachesis Muta's trick would work.

Muta raved on, his voice ringing with hysteria. "It

will be like a chain reaction. First Russia and the United States. But soon the rest of the nuclear powers will get pulled into it, because of treaties they have with the U.S. and the U.S.S.R. Poland, Yugoslavia, England, France—before it's over at least three-quarters of the world will be destroyed. Then, after the smoke and the fallout settle, I, Lachesis Muta, will step in and take control of what is left and reshape it into a perfect society."

How many times had those same words been spoken? Paul wondered. Genghis Khan had wanted to rule the world in ancient China. Napoleon had believed he was the man for the job. Then there was Adolf Hitler, who had come very close to conquering the whole world. However, there was one bright light to be seen in the lessons of history. All of the madmen who had battled and schemed to conquer the world had seen their fantastic dreams go up in smoke. Not one had ever succeeded.

Paul made a vow to himself: Lachesis Muta would not succeed, either. If he did, it would be over the dead body of the Space Eagle!

The first thing to do was to look for some small flaw in Muta's planning. It could not be as foolproof as it sounded. Nothing could be that perfect. Muta was human, a man like any other men. Men made mistakes.

"Tell me, Father," he said casually. "Suppose the news of what you are doing here leaked out to the world? The Americans or the Russians could send bombs and missiles to wipe your mountain off the face of the earth, couldn't they?"

Muta smiled. Obviously he enjoyed having his handiwork challenged. "There is a very small chance of that," he said, "but even if it were so, nothing would change. This entire area of Tibet is ringed with our own supersensitive radar. If bombers or missiles ever threaten our position here, the ICBM's will be automatically activated and triggered by computer."

"I see," Paul said, trying to hide sudden, deep discouragement as he asked a last question. "What would happen if you met with an accident? You could die. Then no one else could enter this control sector to fire the missiles, could they? You said the minds of the security guards have been drugged and programmed to admit only you and Mozzo *together*."

"That's true," Muta admitted. "It would be tragic if anything happened to prevent me from carrying out my noble plans to reorganize this sick world. But even in that event, the first part of the plan would proceed on schedule. The missiles are already programmed to go off at midnight on December twenty-fourth, barring an emergency that would trigger them before that date, as I just explained to you."

Paul felt like pounding his fists on the wall. Every way he turned, he looked down a blind alley. Now he was anxious to get off by himself and contact the President on the button transmitter-receiver concealed within his right ear. Possibly the President would have a suggestion. At any rate, Paul could warn him what to expect, and the President and the Russian Premier could confer on joint measures the two nations could take to foil Dr. Lachesis Muta.

"This is all very interesting, Father," he said, "but I would like to rest for a few hours now."

"Of course," Muta agreed. "You have had a long, hard day, my son." He moved close to Paul and laid a bony hand gently on his arm. "I hope you understand now why I had to have you brought here,

Addison. It was to save your life."

Paul tried to make his voice sound a little more friendly. It was necessary that he win Muta's full confidence, or he would have no chance to stop him at all.

"Yes, Father, I do understand," he said. "But it will take a while before I can completely forgive you for leaving us like that in Tokyo."

Muta smiled. "You will try?"

Paul returned the smile. "I will try." This time he took the older man's hand when he offered it.

"My son," Muta said with satisfaction. "Together we will make a new world."

Paul was escorted to a large, fancy apartment by a small, wrinkled Chinese in green trousers and tunic. "I am to be your servant," he said in singsong English. "My name is Chin."

Paul dismissed him and locked the door. Then he went into the bedroom and shut that door. Sitting down on the bed, he removed the button radio from his ear and broke it apart. With a pin which he always kept on the underside of his shirt collar, he dialed the President's phone number. All he received was deafening static.

Cold dread swept over Paul Girard. Deep inside this mountain, surrounded by rock and steel and all kinds of electronic interference, his little radio was useless. It could not penetrate to the outside world. He could not contact the President nor anyone else. Nor could he signal the S.W.I.F.T. circling silently in its orbit high overhead.

There was no person or thing that he could count on for help. He was all alone. It was the Space Eagle against Dr. Lachesis Muta and his army of slave workers and soldiers!

11.

DISCOVERED!

THE NEXT three days were pure agony for Paul. He had free run of the maze of tunnels and caverns that made up the beehive world inside the mountain, with the exception of the missile control center and the top level, which led to the outside world. Wherever he went, Mozzo, the giant robot, was at his side.

Several times he complained to Muta at mealtime. He never saw the mad doctor except at meals and for a little time at night before they went to bed.

"Why does Mozzo follow me around the way he does?" he asked. "He makes me nervous."

The doctor smiled pleasantly. "I don't want any harm to befall you, my boy. One of the workers or soldiers might take a dislike to you. One can never tell. Mozzo will see to it that you are always safe."

"Does that monster ever run down?" Paul asked one night, with an irritable glance at the robot.

"Oh, Mozzo takes his rest with me," Muta answered casually. "When my brain is asleep, his computer brain is inactivated."

"Is that so?" Paul said. He had a hunch that fact might come in handy to him.

Aside from his impatience at his helplessness as the hours and days rolled past, Paul was uneasy for another reason. He did not believe Muta's explanation about Mozzo. It was his distinct feeling that the robot was not watching out for his *safety*. Mozzo was just watching *him*. If so, it meant that Lachesis Muta did not entirely trust him.

There were other incidents that made him even more suspicious. The doctor talked constantly about the past, questioning him in detail about his life, going all the way back to his boyhood. Paul was ready for him, luckily. His photographic memory had thoroughly digested every fact in the thick FBI files relating to Lachesis Muta and Addison Muta. Yet he had to be on his guard every moment.

On the morning of December 21 something else happened. At the breakfast table, Muta reached into his pocket and handed a small object across the table to Paul. Paul's heart skipped a beat. It was his jeweler's eyepiece, the one he used to magnify the tiny dial of his ear radio!

His voice was calm and casual. "Say, that looks like mine. Where did you get it, Father?"

Muta smiled. "I'm afraid the Chinese servant I gave you is dishonest, Addison. Once a day every man working here is scanned with an electronic detector to see if he is hiding anything that should not be in his possession. This was found on Chin."

Paul laughed. "Well, don't be too hard on him. It isn't very valuable."

Muta chewed his steak thoughtfully. "Whatever do you do with a watchmaker's eyepiece, Addison?"

Paul shrugged. "It's a hobby I picked up in San Francisco. Repairing watches is fun, and it saves me a lot of money."

Muta's eyes glittered. "You must be very hard on your watches, my boy."

Paul laughed, but inside he was not laughing. He would have to be even more alert now than before. Lachesis Muta had a mind as keen as a computer. He had a strong feeling that he could not afford to make one more mistake, even such a small one as leaving the magnifying eyepiece lying around where Muta's spies could get their hands on it.

After they had eaten, Muta went to his office, and Paul trudged back to his apartment with the silent Mozzo shuffling after him. Inside, he threw himself down on the bed and stared at the ceiling. Almost seventeen days had passed since the President had given this urgent assignment to the Space Eagle. Only four days remained until doomsday!

He smiled grimly to himself. It was beginning to look as if the Space Eagle was going to have his wings clipped before he was able to try them!

Later, walking into the dining room for the evening meal, he sensed the unnatural tension. Lachesis Muta was staring, glass-eyed, at his plate.

"Did you have a good day, Father?" Paul asked.

"An excellent day," Muta said. "Our work here in the mountain is finished. Nothing remains to be done except to wait. It is up to the computers now."

"Tell me," Paul said lightly. "Suppose for some reason you decide to change your mind. Could you stop the missiles from being launched on December twenty-fifth?"

"That's a stupid question, Addison!" the doctor snapped.

"Oh, I know that," Paul said laughingly, "but just suppose you did change your mind. Could you stop them?"

"Naturally, there has to be a circuit breaker in the firing mechanism of each of the missiles," Muta admitted. "Not because I might change my mind, but merely to prevent the warhead from detonating by accident in the unlikely event that one of the missiles might fizzle out on its launching pad. We don't want to blow ourselves to kingdom come."

"Naturally." Paul smiled. "If that did happen, how would you deactivate the warhead?"

"Those red buttons underneath the monitoring screens in the control room. They release springs inside the warheads which sever key connections at the lead terminals."

Paul put his knife and fork on his half-empty plate and pushed it aside. Immediately a servant who was posted behind his chair moved to the table to remove the plate. As he picked up the knife and fork, he appeared to stumble and bumped into Paul's chair. The knife and fork in his clenched fist jabbed sharply into the back of Paul's right hand.

Paul gave a little cry of surprise and pain as bright red blood welled up out of a gash in the hand.

The servant leaped back, mumbling frightened apologies. Lachesis Muta got to his feet, shouting angrily.

"Clumsy fool! I ought to have you flogged!"

"Please, Father," Paul objected. "He couldn't help it. It's only a scratch, really." He wrapped the injured hand in a table napkin.

"Just the same, I want one of our medics to have a look at it," Muta insisted. He shouted at the servant. "Send a technician from the medical division up here immediately."

Paul tried to protest again, but Muta would not listen. A white-coated medical corpsman arrived, swabbed the gash with antiseptic, and bandaged it neatly. Then he left, and Muta and Paul had their coffee.

Paul had just refilled his cup from an urn on the table when a uniformed guard entered the room and handed Muta a sealed envelope. He stood at attention at the side of the table as the doctor opened the envelope and took out a slip of paper. Muta read the message. Unexpectedly, his hands began to tremble, and his face turned pale.

Paul frowned. "What is it, Father?" he asked.

Muta sprang to his feet and hurled the paper down on the table. "I've known all along there was something strange about you. Now I have the proof. You're not my son!"

Paul got to his feet slowly, his muscles braced for action. His voice was calm. "That's ridiculous! What is this nonsense all about?"

"That cut on your hand—it was no accident. I wanted to get a sample of your blood. The medical corpsman took it down to the laboratory and analyzed it. Your blood is Type O."

"What of it?"

Muta's voice trembled with rage. "My son, Addison, has a very rare type blood. When he was very young, he was injured and had to have a transfusion. They told me then that he was Type AB. I don't know who you are, but you are not my son!"

Paul was caught, and he knew it. There was no use in pretending any longer. Quick as a cobra, his left arm flashed out at the guard standing by Muta's chair. The heel of his hand hit the man on the side

of the neck in a perfect karate chop. The guard collapsed in an unconscious heap. The laser rifle which had been slung over one shoulder went clattering to the floor. As Paul bent to pick it up, he saw Muta grab a knife from the table and spring at him. He caught the doctor's wrist as the knife was driven down toward his back. Paul twisted his wrist, Muta gasped in pain and dropped the knife. Paul shoved him back against the table and brought up the muzzle of the rifle to cover him.

"Just stand where you are, Dr. Muta," he barked. "You know better than anyone else what this little weapon can do."

Muta remained still as a statue, staring at him with hate-filled eyes. But Paul's victory was a short one. Suddenly he was gripped from behind by two viselike arms. The rifle slipped from his hands, and his arms were pinned to his sides. His breath was crushed out of his lungs, and the room spun dizzily around him.

Through the roaring in his ears, he heard Muta's voice. "Mozzo could break you like a matchstick, but I have willed him not to kill you. I don't want you dead. Not yet!"

Paul felt the robot relax his strangling hold a bit, and air rushed back into his lungs. His head cleared. Muta's leering face was only inches away from his. With his evil, glittering eyes, hooked nose, and pointed beard, the mad doctor looked like Satan himself.

His fingers clawed and probed at Paul's hair and face and throat. "It's not a mask!" he exclaimed. "Real hair, real flesh. Incredible! You could be Addison's twin brother. Who are you? And what did you do with my son?"

A sneer curled up one side of Paul's mouth. "You're supposed to be the genius, Doctor. You figure it out for yourself."

Muta's face turned crimson with rage, and he backhanded Paul hard across the face. "Insolent dog!" he screeched. "There are ways to make you talk, my friend—oriental tortures so fiendish that to hear me tell about them would make your blood freeze."

He hit Paul again. Blood trickled from his mouth and nostrils, but Paul only smiled in brave defiance. "You can torture me to death, Dr. Muta, but my lips will remain sealed. Then you'll never know what happened to your son."

Muta straightened up and took a deep breath to control himself. His lips were a thin, bitter line. "I'll find a way to make you talk, you can be certain of it."

"Never!" Paul said. "Remember, Doctor, if you go through with your diabolical scheme to plunge the world into nuclear war, your son will surely die. He's still in the United States, hidden away where your dirty spies can't get at him."

For a moment he thought he had won, as uncertainty flickered over the satanic face, but it was gone quickly. When the doctor answered him, Paul realized that there was great strength as well as great evil in Lachesis Muta.

"If it must be, it must be," he said bitterly. "Nothing will change me from my vital purpose, even if it means that Addison must die. I told you the day you arrived here that duty has to be put ahead of a man's personal desires. My plans will not be changed. The missiles go off as scheduled. . . . Take him away to the dungeon, Mozzo!"

12.

UNEXPECTED HELP

PAUL WAS locked up in a small, dimly lit cell at the bottom level of Lachesis Muta's underground fortress. The walls and door were made of thick steel. It was escape-proof. Paul knew that. Once again he tried to contact the S.W.I.F.T. on the miniature ear transmitter radio, but it was hopeless. The signal was too weak to penetrate the layers of steel and rock and electronic interference inside the mountain.

Paul Girard was an intelligent man. His position seemed hopeless. There was no logical way for him to foil the doctor's plan for world conquest and mass destruction. The Space Eagle had failed, and there was no way he could even let the President know he had failed.

He looked at his watch. It was the morning of

December 22, he reckoned. He counted the hours remaining. There were only sixty-two more hours until the fatal moment. Muta's ICBM's would go winging away toward their targets in Russia and the United States at midnight on Christmas Eve. Within another hour after that time, the entire world could be at war. By morning all that would be left of the United States, Russia, and probably many other countries would be what Muta laughingly called " a smoking hole in the earth."

Paul buried his face in his hands and sighed. *You can't give up!* An inner voice spoke to him. He sat erect and squared his shoulders. Paul Girard had been in tight scrapes before, many times. The important thing was not to be a quitter. He remembered what his old football coach at college used to say: "Fellows, as long as there's still time on the old clock, anything can happen!"

Paul smiled, remembering the biggest game of his life, in his senior year. The home team had been three points behind, and they were back on their own goal line with time for just one play remaining. Paul, the quarterback, had heaved a desperate, long pass far downfield. The ball had left his fingers

164

seconds before the final gun sounded. A stupendous catch by his left end at midfield plus a dazzling display of broken-field running had turned certain defeat into victory.

Paul lifted his head and felt his blood pumping hard through his veins. There was still time on the old clock. Anything could happen. The Space Eagle was not dead yet!

He removed one shoe, slid back the dummy sole, and removed his talon gun from the secret compartment. He inserted a dart into the firing chamber and slipped the gun into his pocket. A daring plan was forming in his mind.

He walked to the door and pounded with his fists on the steel plates. After a moment a peephole on the other side of the door slid open, and a pair of hard, slanted eyes peered into his cell.

"What do you want?" a guard demanded.

"I have an important message for Dr. Muta," Paul said. "Tell him I'm ready to talk. I'll tell him whatever he wants to know in exchange for my own life. I know a way that his son can still be saved."

The guard nodded and shut the peephole. Paul went back to his cot and sat down to wait for a reply. It came sooner than he expected, out of a grilled loudspeaker over the door, and in the loud triumphant voice of Lachesis Muta. The words echoed off the steel plates of the walls and ceiling.

"I received your message, spy, but it came too late. One hour ago I would have bargained with you in order to save Addison's life. Now there is no need to bargain. My son is safe and on his way here to join me."

"No!" Paul gasped. "That's a lie!"

Muta's insane laughter rang in his ears.

"One of my spies is in your FBI in San Francisco. He found out where they were hiding Addison, in a hunting lodge in the Sierra Mountains. An attack force moved in early this morning and rescued him."

Paul was stunned. He had not counted on this development. A double agent! A traitor! It was unthinkable that there could be a turncoat in the FBI. Yet he had no reason to doubt Muta's word.

"You will be taken care of in due time, my friend," the doctor went on. "But I want you to be alive on Christmas Day to learn of the glorious success of our mission."

There was a loud *click*, and the speaker was cut off.

Paul sank back on the cot and stared at the dial of his wristwatch. With every full sweep of the second hand, the world drew closer to its doom!

Another day passed. Now there were but thirty-eight hours left. Paul paced back and forth in his cell like a restless tiger. "More like a bird in a cage," he thought bitterly. "A caged eagle!"

At midday he was startled by the clanging of the steel door. It swung open with a rusty creak, and there, standing on the threshold, was the real Addison Muta!

"It's amazing!" he exclaimed. "I feel as though I am looking into a mirror. We are identical. I didn't believe it when my father told me about you. I had to see for myself."

Young Muta came into the cell followed by Mozzo, the robot. He frowned at Mozzo and said in a low voice, "My bodyguard, or my keeper. I'm not sure which."

Paul's eyes widened alertly. He was sure he could detect something in Addison Muta's tone, something that was encouraging. He said nothing.

167

"I don't know how they made you look like me. It's fantastic. But I think I can guess what you are and why you came here posing as me," Addison went on. In a whisper, he asked, "Can we talk freely, or is this cell bugged?"

"I don't know," Paul said, indicating the speaker over the door. "I know that's a two-way intercom when it's turned on."

"We had better keep it low, then," the other man said. He looked suspiciously at Mozzo. "What about the robot?"

"It neither speaks nor hears," Paul said. "Its computer brain is merely an extension of your father's brain. His will and desires control its every action."

"He's a remarkable man," Addison said quietly. "What a shame that he's hopelessly mad."

"You know of his plans?"

"Everything. He's got to be stopped! As you must know, I'm not here of my own free will. I was kidnapped from the FBI."

"I know."

The young man's voice was frightened. "What can I do to help? I'd kill him with my own hands if I thought it would help, but it won't. You must

168

know how fiendishly clever he has been about arranging everything."

"Yes," Paul said. "Only he and Mozzo together can get past the security guards into the missile control room. If he dies, the missiles are programmed to go off at midnight of December twenty-fourth in any case."

"I guess it's hopeless, then," Addison moaned.

"Not quite hopeless." Paul's square jaw was as hard as granite. "There's one chance left to us. Not much of a chance, but it is a hope. Do you think you can persuade your father to come down here to see me?"

Addison frowned. "I don't know. I'll try to think of something. What do you have in mind if I can get him down here? Don't forget, this metal monster will probably come with him. It can crush you like a fly if you attack him."

"I'll worry about Mozzo. You bring Lachesis Muta back to this cell."

"I'll do my best." Addison extended his hand and Paul shook it. The young man grinned suddenly. "It feels strange having a twin after all these years. Would you mind telling me how it was done?"

Paul smiled. "Maybe someday, but not for the moment."

Addison's eyes lit up, and he looked thoughtfully at Paul for a moment. Then he exclaimed, "That may be the answer!"

"The answer to what?" Paul asked, puzzled.

"Never mind. We'll soon know if I'm right."

Addison rapped on the steel door, and the guard outside in the corridor opened it to permit him and the robot to leave. Paul lay on his hard cot, counting the hours and minutes—and praying.

The hours passed, and then it was another day. December 24! And still there was no sign of Lachesis Muta or his son Addison. Apparently, Paul thought, young Muta's scheme to lure his father down to the dungeon had failed.

Paul sat on the bare cot, hypnotized by the moving hands of his wristwatch. They met at 12:00 noon. Now there were only twelve hours remaining. The afternoon passed quickly—too quickly. It was 6:00 P.M. Then 7:00 came around. A half hour later Paul was ready to give up at last. The clock was going to run out on him this time. He could feel it in his bones. This time there would be no last-ditch touchdown pass to save the day.

At 7:45 the door of the cell clanged open, and there stood the tall, satanic figure of Dr. Lachesis Muta!

Paul got slowly to his feet as Muta entered the room, followed by Addison and the ever-present robot, Mozzo.

"Good evening," the doctor said with nasty humor. "My son seemed to feel we could learn something valuable by coming here. Personally, I feel it's a waste of time." He laughed. "But it's only right, I suppose, to give the condemned man one final request."

Addison spoke up. "I told my father that you would tell us how you were made to look exactly like me."

"Also who you are and the name of the organization you work for," Muta said.

"With pleasure," Paul said pleasantly. He glanced at the door to make sure it was closed. Then he whipped out his talon gun and aimed it at the mad doctor.

Muta's eyes widened in fear. "Where did you get that weapon?" he hissed. "Before they put you in here, you were screened by the electronic detector."

"Nonmetallic parts," Paul snapped. "Now, Doctor, you want to know who I am? All right, I'll tell you. They call me the Space Eagle!"

"Mozzo, kill him!" Muta shouted.

The robot was already moving swiftly toward Paul, activated by its master's brain cells. Ignoring Mozzo, Paul squeezed off a shot.

The dart hit Muta squarely in the chest. He stared in stunned horror at the strange talon-shaped object embedded in his flesh. An instant later the powerful tranquilizer took effect, and he slumped to the floor with a low moan. Mozzo was almost upon Paul now. The robot's right arm was uplifted, ready to strike. Mozzo took one more step, then stopped suddenly. The lifted arm dropped slowly to its side and swung back and forth loosely a few times like a pendulum.

"How did you manage that?" Addison asked in a shaky voice.

"I put out your father with a tranquilizer dart. I had to gamble on Mozzo. He mentioned once that the robot was inactivated when he was sleeping. They have the same brain, in a manner of speaking."

172

"Yes, I know." Young Muta glanced anxiously toward the door. "What happens now?"

"You'll go outside and keep the guard busy. Tell him your father wants to question me privately. I'll need an hour. Can you manage him?"

"I'll manage him—one way or another," Addison said grimly.

Paul hurriedly exchanged clothing with Lachesis Muta. He placed the doctor's unconscious form on the cot and stood over him with his back to the door. The immobile robot partially concealed him from the angle of the doorway.

"All right," he said. "Knock for the guard. If he doesn't get too good a look at me, I think we can fool him."

The guard didn't even glance at Paul when he let Addison out of the cell. When the door clanged shut, Paul propped up Lachesis Muta on the cot with his back to the wall and went to work.

13.

TOO LATE!

ADDISON MUTA was soaked with perspiration. For almost one hour he had been carrying on a one-sided conversation with the armed guard in the corridor. The man was starting to become suspicious.

"Why is he taking so long in there?" he asked Addison. "Maybe we should look in on them. That prisoner may have done some harm to the doctor."

Addison forced himself to laugh dryly. "Harm my father? With Mozzo at his side? Don't be ridiculous."

"I suppose it's all right," the man said sullenly. "Just the same—"

He was interrupted by a pounding on the door from inside the dungeon. Hastily he threw open the heavy door. Lachesis Muta stepped across the threshold.

"I have finished questioning the prisoner," he said in a voice that, to Addison's ear, sounded somehow different from his father's voice. "I gave him an injection that put him into a deep hypnotic trance. It will be several hours before he recovers. Some people become violent when they come out of it, so I left Mozzo with him to see that he does no harm to himself."

He leered fiendishly at the guard. "I have such marvelous tortures planned for him. It would be a shame if anything happened to him now and spoiled my fun."

The guard giggled unpleasantly. "Yes, sir."

Before the door swung shut, Addison caught a quick glimpse of a figure in the prisoner's clothing sprawled facedown on the cot with Mozzo standing over him.

"Come, my son," the older man said to him. "There is much to be done before midnight."

The two of them started down the corridor in the direction of the elevator. When they were a safe distance away from the guard, Addison stared at the other man in disbelief.

"Is it really you?" he whispered.

"Your father and Mozzo will be out of action for some time," Paul answered in his natural voice.

Addison shook his head. "You must be a sorcerer," he said weakly.

"No," Paul said. "I'm the Space Eagle."

"I don't understand."

"I'll explain as best as I can," Paul said. "You must be patient."

When they were back in Lachesis Muta's quarters on the control level, Paul told Addison Muta as much as he could about his vital assignment without violating security. He did not reveal his true identity as the millionaire playboy tycoon who headed the famous Girard industrial empire.

"Only the President of the United States knows who I am. To everyone else I am the Space Eagle, chief of the United States Spatial Intelligence Agency. Addison, the help and cooperation you have shown me proves, without any doubt, that you are a man of good character and a loyal American. It must have been a very difficult choice for you to make, taking sides against your own father."

Addison Muta's eyes fell. "Please, sir," he said in a low voice, "I'd like to forget that that madman is my father."

"I understand," Paul said with sympathy. He put his hand on the other man's shoulder. "Addison, you've done your part. Now we've got to get you out of here before they find out what you've done."

Young Muta looked up in surprise. "Out of here? What do you mean, Space Eagle?"

"You'll go out the same way you came. By plane. I'll tell the others that I'm sending you on a secret mission to Tokyo."

"But what about you?"

Paul looked at the clock on the wall. It was 9:30 P.M. "I've got to get into the missile room before midnight and push those circuit breakers."

"How will you do it? Even though they'll think you are my father, they won't let you in without Mozzo. Father considered something like this could happen when he set up the security regulations for the control center. The guards will cut you down without mercy if you try to get in without the robot."

"That's a risk I'll have to take."

Addison Muta stood very erect. "I won't do it," he

177

said stubbornly. "I won't leave you to face this alone. After all, he is my father. That makes it my responsibility just as much as yours. If his horrible plan succeeds, I'd just as soon be dead as to live with the knowledge that my father was the fiend who brought it about."

Paul looked at the other man in silent respect for a long time. Then he said, "Addison, I consider it a privilege to have known a man like you, even so briefly—if this *is* our last night on earth."

"Thank you, sir," Muta murmured. "Now, let's get down to business. What are we going to do?"

"Well, since you insist on getting mixed up in this dirty business, Addison, there is a way you can help. It's a long chance, but it's the last chance we have to stop Lachesis Muta from destroying the world."

"Then let's get busy," Addison said.

During his explorations of the mountain fortress, Paul had stumbled on the laboratory where Dr. Muta had created and put together Mozzo the robot. Mozzo was clearly the final product of many experiments. The lab was cluttered with parts of other similar robots, some of them almost completed.

When Paul and Addison entered the lab, the guard at the door stiffened to attention.

Paul spoke to him sharply, imitating the deep, intense voice of the mad doctor. "There is no further need to post a sentry at this door. I told the captain of the guard that last week. You are relieved. Go back to your quarters."

"Yes, *sir,* Dr. Muta," the man said, saluting briskly.

Paul winked at Addison, and they went inside the lab. Paul went to a rack where half a dozen sets of plastic skins similar to the sheathing that covered Mozzo's metal casing were hanging loosely from hooks.

"Have you ever been to a masquerade party, Addison?" he asked lightly.

"Yes, but—"

Paul cut him off. "Do you think you can impersonate Mozzo?"

Addison fingered one of the plastic skins thoughtfully. He saw what the Space Eagle was driving at. "I don't know," he said frankly. "The robot is a good foot taller than I am."

"I think you can get away with it," Paul said

179

with confidence. "Just long enough for us to get from the elevator to the first security chamber." He unhooked one of the plastic sheaths from the rack and handed it to Addison. "Anyway, we have nothing to lose. Give it a try."

It was not as simple as Paul had thought. All of the plastic sheaths in the lab were much too large for Addison's slim frame. They had to cut and trim and patch and pin before one skin was finally fitted to him. Even then his appearance was just passable.

"It's the best we can do," Paul said. "Let's hope those guards won't be looking too closely when we get off the elevator."

It was an easier problem to fit Addison with a pair of black coveralls of the type that the robot wore. When he was finished, Paul stepped back and inspected the other man.

"Not too bad, at that," he said. "Now if you can imitate that stiff, jerky walk of his, we'll be all set to go."

"I think I know a way that will make it seem more realistic," Addison said. "Is there some way we could attach wooden blocks to the soles of my shoes? It would build up my height, and it would make it easier to copy Mozzo's heavy, shuffling gait."

"Good idea," Paul agreed. They rummaged through a trash box in one corner of the room and came up with a short length of a two-by-four beam. With a saw he found on the workbench, Paul cut off two blocks that were slightly shorter than Addison's boots. Addison removed his boots, and they nailed the blocks to the bottoms of the soles.

"That's fine," Paul said with satisfaction when Addison finished lacing up his built-up footwear and stood up. He was now several inches taller than Paul, and he seemed even taller when Paul walked with a slouch and bent knees.

It was 11:15 P.M.

"Not a moment to waste," Paul said as they emerged from the lab. The corridor was deserted except for a lone guard far down at the steel doors that opened into the central chamber.

The elevator that took them down to the missile control level had red sliding doors with a warning painted across them in white block letters: OFF LIMITS TO ALL BUT AUTHORIZED PERSONNEL IN MISSILE CONTROL SECURITY.

They boarded it and Paul pushed the yellow button marked "MC." There was a sinking feeling in his stomach as the car dropped swiftly.

He looked at Addison. "This is it," he said.

Addison's voice was tense. "I hope my acting holds up."

Paul patted him on the shoulder. "You'll be all right. You ought to see yourself. You make a fine robot, really."

Addison laughed grimly. Then the two men faced the front of the car in silence. It came to a stop with a gentle bump, and the doors slid apart. Paul and Addison stared into a ring of grim, cold faces on the circular balcony suspended ten feet above the rough stone floor. Laser rifles were trained on them from all sides.

Paul's legs and feet wanted to cover the long walk to the steel door opposite the elevator as fast as possible, but he forced himself to walk at a slow and leisurely pace with Addison shuffling along a few steps behind in his stiff robot's gait.

The corporal of the guard stood with both hands on the balcony railing just above the steel door. He glanced down at the two figures briefly. Then he

turned and pushed a green button on a panel behind him. It was the signal for the guards in the inner chamber to open the door. The steel panel slid open with a faint whirring sound.

"We made it!" Paul said softly.

He stepped inside the smaller chamber quickly, followed by Addison. There was a guard posted on either side of the next door, each with a laser rifle slung carelessly over his shoulder. In the center of the steel door was a small panel with two buttons on it—one red, the other green.

The guards looked them over. Then one of them reached for the panel and put a finger on the green button. Paul held his breath as the finger hesitated. The man was a stocky Chinese with a waxed moustache that drooped at the ends. His slanted eyes narrowed, and he looked back at Paul. His gaze turned to Addison, and he scowled.

He spoke sharply to the other guard in Chinese, and his hand darted toward the red button. Paul was too fast for him. A lightning-fast karate chop broke the guard's wrist before he could push the button. His howl of pain died in his throat as Paul hit him again with a hard uppercut on the point of the jaw.

The man slammed back against the wall and slid down to the rock floor, unconscious.

The second guard brought up his rifle, but before he could squeeze the trigger, Paul caught him in the throat with a dart from the talon gun. He was paralyzed instantly as the fast-acting drug stunned his nerves and muscles. A moment later he collapsed on the floor, limp as a rag doll.

Paul whistled between his teeth. "That was a close one."

Addison looked at the next door anxiously. "What about the other guards? Do you think they heard anything?"

"I doubt it," Paul said coolly. "Not with all this steel and rock around us and the noise of motors."

He picked up one of the fallen guard's laser rifles and handed it to Addison. "We may have to fight our way through the next two chambers. Be ready to use this if you have to. Okay, keep your fingers crossed."

He took a deep breath and pressed the green button that would signal "all clear" to the guards within the next chamber.

The time was 11:40 P.M.

The steel door slid open, and they faced two more of Lachesis Muta's surly security guards. They looked impassively at Paul and Addison, fooled by their skillful disguises. Then one of them spotted the two guards crumpled on the floor in the room behind. He cried out and whipped his rifle off his shoulder, but Paul was too quick for him. The talon gun popped softly, and a dart buried itself deep in his right shoulder.

As he fell, Paul turned the talon gun on the other guard, who was fumbling desperately to bring his rifle into action. To Paul's horror, the talon gun misfired!

Addison Muta knew what he had to do. He squeezed the trigger of the laser rifle. Its pencil-thin beam of brilliant ruby light drilled a round, bloodless hole through the man's chest.

"I'm sorry we had to do that," Paul said as he gazed down at the dead man.

"I had no other choice," Addison said grimly. "Come on; it's only twelve minutes until midnight."

Paul pushed the button that would admit them to the third and final chamber. This time he didn't wait for the door to open fully before he opened fire with the talon gun. One guard went down without knowing what had hit him, but Paul had bad luck with his second shot. The little talon-shaped dart struck the stock of the other guard's rifle as he swung it down in front of his body, and it ricocheted off harmlessly.

Paul leaped back out of the doorway as the guard sent a laser lightning bolt streaking at the spot where he had been standing.

"I'll get him!" Addison shouted.

At close range, young Muta and the Chinese guard exchanged fire with the laser rifles. When the brief, furious exchange was over, both men lay sprawled out on the stone floor. The guard was dead, Addison was dying.

Paul knelt down beside young Muta. "You saved my life," he said simply.

Addison waved a hand at the double steel doors behind Paul. His eyes were becoming glassy. "Go . . . hurry . . . the control room. . . ." His voice faltered. "You only have . . . two minutes left."

Paul took Addison's hand and pressed it. "In spite of your father's crimes, there will never be any disgrace on the name of Muta. I'll see to that."

187

From his pocket he took a small silver medallion with an eagle embossed on its face. He placed it in Addison's hand and closed his fingers over it.

"I make you my first deputy—a 'talon of the Space Eagle,' you might say. Good-bye, my friend." He stood up and turned to the last barrier separating him from the control room.

Only sixty seconds were left!

Sweat beaded Paul's forehead. The doors opened with maddening slowness.

Thirty seconds!

He squirmed through the parting doors before they were fully open and dashed to the control panel where the thirteen luminous television monitoring screens showed the deadly missiles in their silos. He jammed the heels of his hands against two of the red circuit breakers under the first two screens. He reached for the next two buttons, but before he could hit them, he froze in horror and despair. It was too late! The remaining eleven ICBM's were hidden as fire and exhaust vapors blotted out the TV screens. The Space Eagle had failed at the last second.

There was nothing anyone could do now to stop

them from blasting off. He watched, stunned, as the big "birds" lifted gracefully out of their silos.

Everything had been in vain, including the death of Addison Muta. Dr. Lachesis Muta had won, after all. His evil would destroy the United States—and maybe the whole world!

14.

BEYOND THE
SPACE-TIME BARRIER

PAUL WATCHED helplessly as the computer that monitored the missiles' guidance systems went into action. A bank of lights on its face flashed on like a theater marquee, spelling out vital statistics: TWENTY-EIGHT MINUTES TO TARGETS.

Twenty-eight minutes to targets, Paul thought. Well, the clock had not run out yet. There was still time. Time for what? He looked around the control room, without knowing exactly what he was looking for. His eye was drawn to a large pipe, about three feet in diameter, that ran up through the floor and ceiling in one corner of the room. From its metal grille came a loud swooshing of air.

"Must be the main ventilation shaft," he said to himself.

He walked over to the pipe and kicked out the grille. Poking his head inside the opening, he squinted up. If his hunch was correct, the shaft went all the way up to the surface. There was a steel-runged ladder fixed to the side of the pipe for the use of workmen when the ventilation system needed repairs. Paul hauled himself through the opening and started to climb.

Ten minutes later he reached the top, emerging into a dim cavern whose walls and floor were made of solid, glistening ice. He looked straight into the muzzles of two laser rifles held by a pair of guards.

Paul decided there was only one thing to do—bluff it out. He climbed out of the shaft and brushed off his dusty clothing.

"Very good, men. You're alert. If I had caught you napping, I would have had your heads."

Startled, the guards looked at each other and then back at Paul. One of them shined a flashlight into his face and gasped in surprise.

"Dr. Muta!"

Thinking quickly, Paul replied in the sharp voice of Lachesis Muta, "Just conducting a sneak inspection to make sure everybody is alert."

In a gesture of friendliness that shocked the guards, he moved between them and put an arm around the shoulders of each. "I'm going to see that you two are rewarded for your vigilance, men," he said.

The two men grinned, unaware of his hands reaching slyly up to the backs of their necks. Suddenly Paul gripped each of them by the nape of the neck and slammed their heads together like a pair of cymbals. There was a loud *konk,* and they slipped down to the icy floor.

Paul glanced at his watch. The missiles had been on their way for fourteen minutes. Only fourteen more to go!

If he could reach the S.W.I.F.T. and bring it down here on the mountaintop, there was still a slim chance. He removed the button radio from his ear and dialed the call letters that would summon the amazing spacecraft from any place in its orbit around the earth. If the signal got through, the auto-pilot computer was programmed to track his directional radio beam and touch down in a maximum time of five minutes. When he finished dialing, he held his breath. One second . . . two seconds. . . .

Then he heard it: two bell-like *beeps!* The S.W.I.F.T.'s computer was signaling back. Here on the high mountain, in the clear air, free of the interference inside the beehive, his SOS had gotten through!

Confident and excited, Paul put through another call to Washington, D.C.

The President's voice, answering, was full of anxiety. "Who is it?"

"Space Eagle here . . . seventy-six sixty," Paul said.

The President's relief was apparent in his voice. "Good Lord! What have you been doing? It's been days since we heard from you. I had just about given up hope."

"Sorry, sir. There was no way I could get through to you. Mr. President, please don't say anything else. Just listen. We don't have much time. Any minute now NORAD will be picking up a formation of unidentified flying objects on the radar coming toward the United States from over the North Pole. They're for real, sir. ICBM's with nuclear warheads."

There was an explosive exclamation at the other end. "Russian missiles?"

"No, that's the point. Just about now, too, the

Russians will be picking up the same thing on their radar. It's a diabolical plot to trick the U.S. and the U.S.S.R. into a destructive nuclear war. The work of Dr. Lachesis Muta."

"If the missiles are already on their way, there's nothing we can do to stop them," the President said in agony.

"The game isn't over yet, sir," Paul said grimly. "I have an idea that may save the day. It's one in a million, but it is a chance."

"Then get on with it, my boy! Is there anything I can do at this end?"

"Yes, get the Russian Premier on the hot line and try to persuade him to sit tight. Convince him that it's a plot to send the two most powerful nations on earth tearing at each other's throats. You've got to stop him from panicking when those missiles head for Moscow, stop him from pushing the button for a massive retaliatory attack."

"I'll do my best, Space Eagle," the President promised.

"So will I, sir," Paul said and broke off the conversation.

He walked to the mouth of the icy cave and

peered out into the snow and mist that shrouded the dark mountain peak, searching for some sign of the S.W.I.F.T.

Through an interpreter, the President of the United States pleaded with the Premier of Russia.

"Mr. Premier, you've got to believe me. Those blips on your radar are *not* United States ICBM's. It's a trick to make us go to war."

The Premier was just as upset as the President. "You sound sincere, Mr. President. I want to believe you, but my military advisers keep saying that it could be an American trick to put us off our guard."

"I know," the President groaned. "My advisers keep telling me the same thing. But the final decision is up to us. We have to trust each other. I trust you; won't you trust me? Sir, do you know what day this is? Christmas! You know what Christmas means to the U.S.A. 'Peace on earth, goodwill toward men.' You must know us Americans better than that, Mr. Premier. We'd never launch a sneak attack on any nation on this day, of all days."

The Premier hesitated. Finally he said, "I believe

you, Mr. President. We will hold back and wait."
A note of irony crept into his voice. "We will wait
for this Christmas miracle you promise us."

At that same moment Paul Girard, in the
S.W.I.F.T., was climbing high above the earth's atmosphere on the trail of the eleven deadly missiles
of Dr. Muta. There were just five minutes remaining
before they curved down from outer space and
blasted their targets in Russia and the United States.
Only one thing could prevent that from happening
—that part of Einstein's Special Theory of Relativity
which dealt with the "battle of the clocks." If the
S.W.I.F.T. could reach the speed of light, 186,282
miles per second, in an orbit around the earth, then
time would, according to Julie's calculations, literally stop!

Paul throttled up the conventional atomic engine
to its peak. He felt the ship tremble as he shifted
over to the matter-antimatter overdrive.

Around and around the earth whipped the
S.W.I.F.T., building up speed with every revolution. The speed gauge needle went crazy. One
thousand miles a second . . . ten thousand miles a

second . . . fifty thousand miles a second.

Once again, Paul went over in his mind the basic reasons why Julie was so certain that Einstein was right. Julie was certain there could be no speed greater than the speed of light. That had been proven in scientific laboratories by shooting electrons and protons and other minute particles through long tunnels, called linear accelerators, at speeds approaching the speed of light. An amazing thing was discovered in these experiments. At 93,000 miles per second, half the speed of light, these particles were foreshortened in the direction of their flight by fifteen percent and their mass increased by the same percentage.

He translated it into an image that was easier for the human brain to understand. If, for example, a foot-long ruler was traveling past a fixed observer at 93,000 miles per second, it would appear to him to be only about ten inches long. But since its weight would remain the same, its mass—the density of the molecules that make it up—would be more compact.

At seven-eighths the speed of light, 163,000 miles per second, the ruler would seem to be only six inches long, and its mass would be twice the mass of the same ruler at rest.

Carried to the ultimate limit, the speed of light itself, the length of the ruler would be zero, and its mass would be infinite. Therefore, Julie had explained to Paul, nothing can travel faster than the speed of light, because there is no length shorter than zero and no mass greater than infinity.

As Julie had also pointed out to him, the risks of trying to break the space-time barrier were great. If the S.W.I.F.T. succeeded in outracing light itself —attained a speed greater than 186,282 miles per second—it might simply vanish in the vast unchartered sea of space and time on the outer limits of the universe.

Paul Girard, the Space Eagle, no longer had any choice. If the world was to be saved from destruction, he would have to dive headfirst into the great black unknown where no man before him had ever been, nor ever, in his wildest nightmares, dreamed of going.

He advanced the red overdrive throttle, and the speed gauge hit one hundred thousand miles per second. It was at this speed that he first noticed the strange thing that was happening to the earth. As he viewed it in the S.W.I.F.T.'s scanning television screens, it seemed flatter on one side than on the other, and smaller. The hairs at the back of his neck prickled with excitement. The earth was contracting, getting smaller, foreshortening on one side so that it was shaped like an ellipse instead of a circle! Here was positive proof! Einstein had been right. Julie was right.

He looked at his watch. In another sixty seconds the missiles would dive on their targets. He ran the throttle all the way up, and saw the needle leap from 150,000 to 160,000.

Up until 150,000 miles per second, Paul had the illusion that the S.W.I.F.T. was suspended absolutely motionless in space. As the needle continued to climb, he was aware of a growing tremor and an uncomfortable, high-pitched, whistling whine in his ears. Now the S.W.I.F.T. was shaking from nose to tail so violently that Paul could not read the dials on the control panel. His vision was blurred. His teeth were chattering with the vibration. The whistling whine became higher and higher pitched until it seemed to pierce his eardrums with hot needles. It was unbearable. Paul closed his eyes and covered his ears with his hands to blot out the awful sound, but it was useless.

His brain was vibrating like a tuning fork. He felt everything slipping away from him as if he were on the verge of blacking out.

Abruptly there was a sharp explosion that seemed to come from all around him, and the S.W.I.F.T. was tumbling over and over in space. Consciousness left him briefly. Then his eyes sprang open. The noise, the vibration, and the discomfort were all gone. Once more the S.W.I.F.T. seemed to be floating motionless in space. His eyes widened as they fell on the speed gauge.

The needle held steady at 187,000 miles per second! He was traveling more than seven hundred miles a second faster than the speed of light! At first he couldn't believe it. *Something must be wrong with the speed gauge,* he thought. He fed some data into the computer, and the answer flashed instantly on its screen: 187,000 miles per second.

With one hand on the speed throttle and the other on the guidance controls, he began to put the second part of his plan into operation. Holding his breath, be brought back the throttle a hairbreadth. The speed dropped off to 186,500 miles per second. It was still too fast. He worked at it until the needle held steady at exactly 186,290 miles per second. Now the S.W.I.F.T. was traveling just eight miles per second above the speed of light.

Then he flipped on the ship's radioactivity detector beam and shifted over to automatic pilot. The time deadline had passed by over four minutes ago, according to the ship's maser clocks. By now the missiles should have done their fiendish work. New York; Washington, D.C.; and Moscow should all be smoking ruins. Paul was no longer worried. He had complete faith in Albert Einstein and Julie Girard.

When the S.W.I.F.T. broke through the space-time barrier, had time stopped for the earth below, for Lachesis Muta's missiles? He would know for sure very shortly.

They appeared first on the nose monitoring screen, six specks in V-formation like flying geese. Gently he cut back the throttle until the needle hung almost on 186,282. He felt the ship begin to tremble and locked it at that speed. If he went any slower, the S.W.I.F.T. would be sucked into the mysterious and turbulent vortex that formed the space-time barrier. The six ICBM's loomed up in the viewing screen; then they were gone again. His rate of speed in relation to the missiles and the earth below was still too great for him to maneuver in close to them. They kept flashing off and on the screen in a blur as the S.W.I.F.T. continued to circle the earth.

There was no hurry anymore. Lachesis Muta's missiles were suspended motionless in time and space for as long as he maintained a speed greater than the speed of light. He could take the time now to perform a few experiments in the interest of science. It was the least he could do for Julie after all she had done for him and for the whole of mankind. It was Julie's creation, the S.W.I.F.T., which had saved the world from going over the brink of nuclear destruction.

One thing bothered him, and he knew it would bother his sister. According to Einstein, there could be no speed greater than the speed of light. But Paul had seen the proof of it on the speed gauge and had verified it on the computer. So Einstein was wrong! Or was he? An idea came to Paul.

The next time the missiles appeared in the cross hairs of the viewing screen he snapped a photograph with the computer's infrared camera eye. The computer then fixed the position of the missiles in relation to the earth below them and to the star Polaris, sixty degrees to their port side. Six times he snapped the same photograph when the S.W.I.F.T. made its passes around the earth. Then he fed the six pictures into the computer's navigation data analysis slot. The results were earthshaking! They cast a whole new light on Einstein's Theory of Relativity and the riddles of time and space.

Einstein was right after all! There was no speed faster than the speed of light. Time *did* stop at the speed of light. The Old Master had simply not gone far enough into the subject. What actually happened when the S.W.I.F.T. broke the time-space barrier was that time *had stopped, and then reversed itself!* The photographs of the missiles showed that they were slowly but surely moving backward, like a movie film running in the wrong direction.

It was a new dimension, a new world. The clocks and gauges of the world as he knew it were useless.

In this world, on the far side of the space-time barrier, the clocks ran backward.

In the future, he and Julie would explore this world more carefully, but now Paul was concerned with his own world.

On his next pass around the earth, he trained the electronic sights of the laser cannon on the missile formation and pulverized the warhead of one of them. He continued to blast them with the laser cannon until all that was left of the six missiles was a heap of scrap metal drifting about in space.

Now he altered the S.W.I.F.T.'s orbit to look for the remaining five missiles that were menacing the Soviet Union. He located them easily with the radioactivity detector beam and soon turned them into junk as well.

When it was done, Paul smiled wryly and said to himself, "It's a lucky thing there isn't a space police force right now. Sure as shooting, I'd be given a summons for littering."

Paul felt very good. On his first assignment as the chief of the United States Spatial Intelligence Agency, the Space Eagle had turned almost certain defeat into victory. Dr. Lachesis Muta and his forces of evil

had lost their bid to conquer the world. It was time to go back to the world where he belonged.

Paul pushed the red handle of the matter-antimatter engine back slowly. The needle of the speed gauge fell back to 186,282 miles per second. The S.W.I.F.T. began to buck and shudder like an old Model T going over a bumpy dirt road. His vision blurred. There was a loud explosion, and once again the ship began to tumble end over end. Paul blacked out.

When he came to, he was aware of the terrible, shrill whistling in his ears. Only this time, the high pitch fell off rapidly, and in less than a minute it faded away altogether.

Paul took a deep breath and shook his head to clear it. The speed gauge read 100,500 miles per second and was going down, down, down. Things were back to normal once more.

He put through a call to the White House on the S.W.I.F.T.'s wireless radio. The President answered immediately.

"Space Eagle here," Paul said crisply. "Seventy-six sixty. . . ."

"Thank heaven!" the President said in relief. "I

just finished talking to the Russian Premier. All of a sudden the missiles vanished from our radarscopes. It was like a miracle."

"You could call it that, sir," Paul replied.

"How did you manage it?" the President demanded.

Paul gave a shaky laugh. "Mr. President," he said, "if I told you, you wouldn't believe it. In any event, the crisis is over. We have nothing more to fear from Lachesis Muta's plot."

"How can you be sure of that?" the President asked.

"As soon as I hang up, I'm making sure of it," Paul said grimly. "Good night, sir. And don't worry."

He put the S.W.I.F.T. on autopilot and fed the map coordinates of Muta's Tibetan stronghold into the directional computer. Minutes later the S.W.I.F.T. was hovering directly over the snow-covered mountain dome that contained the mad doctor's hive.

Paul flicked on the infrared scanner and studied the terrain below. Dark patches that had been invisible to the naked eye showed up on the snow.

He knew they marked the location of air shafts, concealed exits, and other openings from which the heat generated in the underground city was escaping to the surface.

On a long, steep slope on the north side of the mountain, he discovered what he was looking for —thirteen round, dark circular patches, all in a neat row. These marked the location of the missile silos. He swooped low over the patches, scanning them with the ship's Geiger counter. The meter chattered wildly as the S.W.I.F.T. passed over the last two silos. At the bottom of these shafts were the two ICBM's he had managed to deactivate.

Paul backed off to a height of thirty miles and trained the laser nose cannon on one of the dark patches on the mountainside. It would only take one shot to do the job.

Carefully he adjusted the cannon's power scale, so that the laser beam would not demolish the missile. He wanted just enough force to detonate the warhead. When the electronic gunsight flashed the "On Target" signal, Paul squeezed the trigger. It was as simple as shooting fish in a rain barrel.

A sheet of flame obscured the ground. Then the

ship went bounding ever higher into the sky on the shock wave. Paul watched the familiar mushroom cloud climbing into the air after him. He smiled with grim satisfaction. It was possible that Lachesis Muta and his henchmen had fled in the minutes since Paul had escaped, but his insane dream had gone up in a puff of smoke—smoke from the bombs he had created with his own hand to enslave the world.

On seismographs around the world, the tremor would be regarded as just one more earthquake from that desolate part of the earth.

15.

PLAUDITS

PAUL RETURNED to the Girard Foundation with some priceless gifts for Julie, the magnetic memory tapes from the S.W.I.F.T.'s computers. She would not have traded them for many times their weight in precious jewels.

"The data on those tapes have pushed scientific research ahead by at least twenty years, Paul," she said. "Imagine, positive proof that Einstein's Special Theory of Relativity is right to the last detail. Even the 'battle of the clocks' settled once and for all."

Paul smiled. "The only trouble is, sis, we can't release this information to the world. If we did, we'd have to tell everyone how we got the proof. That would mean revealing the secret power of the S.W.I.F.T."

Julie suddenly looked glum. "I forgot about that," she said. "We can't risk the Russians getting their hands on the spartanium engine plans."

"Someday, maybe, but not now. Better store your tapes and data in the Top Security Three Vault, along with the formulas for instant plastic surgery and all our other discoveries that this mixed-up world isn't ready for yet."

He yawned. "Now I think I'll drive down to Paradise Valley and sleep for a week."

Julie laughed. "You rate it, big brother. And I do mean 'big.'"

Paul patted her arm fondly. "Thanks, squirt."

About one week later, Paul Girard received a formal engraved invitation from the White House to attend a concert and a buffet supper. Naturally he accepted.

When the President greeted him in the official receiving line, he gave Paul only a brief "hello" and a curt nod. Later, as Paul was inspecting a painting on the wall in a far corner of the room, the Chief Executive drifted over to him and whispered out of the corner of his mouth:

"The Space Eagle saved humanity. A wonderful triumph over the forces of evil. The whole world is in your debt, Paul."

"I couldn't have accomplished it without the aid of Addison Muta. He gave his life to foil his father's plans."

"Yes, he was a brave and honorable man."

Paul sighed. "I don't mind telling you, Mr. President, I wouldn't want another mission as tough as this one."

The President's eyes twinkled. "Don't count on it, my boy. I have a hunch that the Space Eagle will be spreading his wings again very, very soon."

Paul took a deep breath and squared his broad shoulders.

THE SPACE EAGLE
PLEDGE TO AMERICA

I believe that *all* men are created equal and that they are endowed by their Creator with certain inalienable rights, among which are life, liberty, and the pursuit of happiness. I believe that recognition of this equality, and of these rights, is every man's personal responsibility.

It is with these beliefs that I on my most sacred honor pledge my allegiance to the United States of America, the land of the free and the home of the brave, being fully aware that such nation shall continue to be the land of the free only so long as it shall remain the home of the brave.

May God bless the U.S.A.

Whitman ADVENTURE and MYSTERY Books

Adventure Stories for GIRLS and BOYS...

New Stories About Your Television Favorites...

BRAINS BENTON SERIES
The Missing Message
The Counterfeit Coin
The Stolen Dummy

DONNA PARKER
In Hollywood
Special Agent
On Her Own
A Spring to Remember
Takes a Giant Step

POWER BOYS SERIES
The Haunted Skyscraper
The Flying Skeleton
The Burning Ocean
The Million-Dollar Penny
The Double Kidnapping
The Vanishing Lady

REAL LIFE STORIES
To Dance, To Dream
Heroes in Blue and Gray

Bonanza

The Man From U.N.C.L.E.
The Gentle Saboteur
The Gunrunners' Gold

F Troop

The Gnome-Mobile

Lassie
Secret of the Summer
Blackberry Bog
Bristlecone Pine

I Spy

The Munsters
The Last Resort

Gilligan's Island

The Big Valley

The Green Hornet

Tarzan

Walt Disney's Annette